A CHARMED DEATH

A CHARMED DEATH

MILES TRIPP

St. Martin's Press
New York

Library of Congress Cataloging in Publication Data

Tripp, Miles, 1923-
    A charmed death.

    I. Title.
PR6070.R48C46   1984   823'.914   84-18351
ISBN 0-312-13076-7

First published in Great Britain by Macmillan London Ltd.

First U.S. Edition

10 9 8 7 6 5 4 3 2 1

A CHARMED DEATH

Part 1

ONE

Stella Best was thirty years old when she discovered a truth which lucky people never discover. It is the truth that peace of mind once shattered can never be completely restored. On the morning when she last had peace of mind she and her husband, Rodney, were at their cottage near the Suffolk coast. She liked to describe it as 'a place to get away from it all' not realising that she had little to get away from and that one day she would want desperately to get away from the cottage.

It had rained overnight but the sky was clearing and, looking out of the window at ragged patches of blue, Rodney said, 'It'll be a lovely day. I'd like to get in nine holes before I go.' Ruefully he added, 'I envy you, staying on.'

'I've changed my mind,' she said.

He turned from the window, startled. 'Changed your mind?'

'I think I'll come home with you. I've got things to do before the new term starts.'

She was a teacher at a comprehensive school.

'Well, you don't mind, do you?' she asked with a smile.

'Of course not. It was just that I thought . . .'

He didn't say what he thought and she finished the sentence for him. 'You thought you were going to be off the lead for three or four days.'

'That's right. Living it up. Orgies and debauchery with

Robinson of Accounts and Fred Hannay of Buying.'

He and Stella had been married for seven years and if separately asked about their marriage would have given an identical answer – good.

'You go and play golf then,' she said. 'I'll take Max for a walk and then clear up. There's not much to do.'

At the mention of its name an old black labrador which spent more time asleep than awake stood up, stretched, and wagged its tail.

'You don't want the car?' he asked. Sometimes he walked the mile and a half to the golf course and sometimes he drove there.

'You take it,' she said. They had come in her Volvo hatchback and left his company car at home.

Minutes later Stella was striding across the common, breathing in the scents of damp earth and rain-freshened gorse and heather. A rabbit zig-zagged across her path and Max made a token effort at pursuit but soon returned to lollop at her heels. Stella loved the unspoiled heathland which was bordered by pine woods beyond which were sand-dunes and the sea. And she loved the little nineteenth century cottage which stood at one end of the common and was close to a wood where nightingales sang and wild creatures found sanctuary.

The cottage could only be reached by a rutted track. Water had to be drawn from a well and there was no main drainage. However, the previous owner had laid on electricity and converted an adjacent storehouse into a very large garage. It was a square and ugly brick building with an up-and-over self-locking metal door; a heavily-barred window in one wall gave the impression that it was a jail but the bars had been fixed to keep out thieves. The previous owner had a passion for reconstructing vintage cars and feared irreplaceable parts might be stolen. Sometimes Stella and Rodney toyed with the idea of converting the garage into a habitable annexe but never got around to having plans prepared.

Their nearest neighbour was Mrs Prentice, a widow who lived with three cats half a mile away at the point where the track joined a lane which led to golf links and the sea. She had keys to the cottage and was caretaker while they were in London.

Stella and Max had reached a strip of land which bisected the common. It had once been the site of a railway track but when uneconomic branches had been axed the line had been closed, rails and sleepers removed, and now only the green scar of a grassy track remained. As always when she came to this part of the common Stella looked both ways as if to make sure a ghost train wasn't rattling down invisible lines.

For a few moments she stood still, breathing deeply air which had been freshened by the tang of sea breezes blowing through pines. Without being aware of it, she was completely at peace. In weeks to come she was to recollect these moments of peace; grass, gorse, broom and heather spreading out in all directions and Max standing beside her, his greying muzzle lifted as if hopeful that some once familiar but now half-forgotten smell of rabbit would waft his way.

'We must get back,' she said aloud. The tranquil spell was broken. It was time to think what should be packed and what should be left for the next visit.

When Rodney returned to the cottage he complained that his swing had been wrong. 'I wish I could stay a bit longer and have some coaching from the club pro. He's a good chap.'

She paused from emptying a bowl of sugar into a plastic container. 'Could you stay on if you wanted?'

'Not a chance. Conference at Romford tomorrow.'

He was regional sales manager for a food manufacturing company called Susan's Starters plc.

'Monday? I thought Romford conferences were always on Thursdays.'

'It's an extra one. Storage problems have cropped up. I

have to be there, but I don't know why you can't stay. It'd do you good.'

She was amused. 'I don't need doing good to.'

'I could come up mid-week as originally planned and collect you.'

'Thanks. But I don't want to stay. I've said, I've got things to do.'

He feigned a smile. 'Fine.'

'If you're not careful I shall think you don't want me home. There really is an orgy on your mind.'

He feigned puzzlement. 'Georgia on my mind?'

'I said "orgy", you fool.'

'You're right. There is. And not only on my mind. The typing pool will be bitterly disappointed when I say it's all off. Miss Standish will be devastated. She's even bought herself a see-through nightie for the thrash.' He became suddenly thoughtful. 'Perhaps she'd lend it to us.'

'I don't want a see-through nightie,' she said sharply.

'Not for you, dearest! It's for me!'

'Ha ha,' she said slowly. 'Very funny.'

She didn't share his sense of humour when it came to jokes about sexual ambiguity. Nor did she care much for discussions about sex. For her, this was a subject requiring a minimum of dialogue and then only between husband and wife in a darkened bedroom. Sex was an intimate physical transaction which took place preferably at lengthening intervals even though on rare occasions, she had found bodily contact pleasurable. Not that she ever went further than saying it was 'quite nice' or 'not bad' before turning on her side and remarking it was high time for sleep or 'we shan't be very bright in the morning'.

But if they were less than perfectly compatible in the sexual side of married life they cared about each other and if, as she sometimes wondered, he had brief infidelities when away on business he was careful to maintain a discreet silence. She never doubted his loyalty to her and this was a condition far more important than mere physical fidelity. And anyway, she knew him well enough to be convinced that if any transient affair became too hot to handle he would run for safety.

They left the cottage after a light snack. Although it was her car Rodney had said he would like to drive and she agreed. At the end of the track they stopped to tell Mrs Prentice they were leaving but hoped to be back before long.

The distance between the cottage and their home in a suburb of north London was roughly a hundred miles. Usually they travelled by the main A11 highway but for variety sometimes took a diversion through the Suffolk countryside. Today Rodney decided to take the diversion.

It was a fine afternoon in early spring and hedges and trees were beginning to burst with new life as tiny buds sprang their slow-motion explosions of freshest green. Cocooned in the car Stella enjoyed the fleeting changes of scenery and later remembered little of the sporadic conversation she'd had with Rodney except that at one point he'd said something about acupuncture and that perhaps he'd give it a try in an attempt to give up smoking.

Her lips had curled in a wry smile. About three times a year he gave up smoking, became intensely irritable, and then resumed the habit after a break of less than a week.

'You have been smoking rather a lot,' she commented.

'On second thoughts,' he went on, 'I won't try acupuncture. Can't risk the needle going in the wrong place and puncturing my ego by mistake.' He laughed and immediately lighted a cigarette.

For a while they travelled in silence and then suddenly he said, 'Max is very restive. Maybe he wants to do his duty.'

11

She turned to look. During journeys the dog occupied the space between the back seat and the hatchback door. He was out of sight.

'I can't see him,' she said.

'He's sitting down now. But I've been watching in the mirror and he's been moving about. I think he needs to be let out.'

As a rule Rodney didn't like interrupting a journey and Stella expected him to say, 'If he's settled, we'll press on.' Instead he said, 'We'll look for somewhere suitable.'

'What about there?' She pointed to a lay-by ahead.

Perhaps he had been driving too fast because he said something about a car being right behind them and the danger of braking. But a minute later he pulled into the verge. 'This'll do.' He switched off the engine. 'No need for you to come. We shan't be a moment.'

'I'll come too.'

'Hardly worth it,' he said in a clipped voice.

'I'd like to stretch my legs. It's a nice afternoon and we're not in a mad rush to get home, are we?'

He turned to get out of the car. 'Of course not,' he said, speaking over his shoulder. He sounded annoyed and she wondered if she'd said something wrong.

He let Max out of the back and they set off into what seemed to be a thickly wooded copse.

Brambles clawed at her slacks. 'This isn't much of a place for a dog walk,' she said, only to find he had forced his way through a clump of ground elder and was almost out of sight. 'Hold on,' she called, pulling herself free from the brambles.

There was no reply. He had disappeared from view. She stood, undecided whether to return to the car or follow him. A spasm of annoyance crossed her face transforming it from the pert prettiness inherited from her mother to the firm-jawed mien of her father. She thrust through nettles and brambles in the direction he had taken, ducking her head to avoid an overhanging

12

sycamore branch. And then she saw him on the other side of a small clearing. He was holding Max's collar and seemed to be peering into a thicket.

It might have been the tension in his body posture, or a sixth sense on her part, but she had a strong premonition that something was badly amiss. She hurried forward. 'What is it?'

He straightened up. 'Don't look. It's a body. Max found it.'

She did look. Flat-heeled shoes on two slender legs which were bent at the knees. A green tweed skirt rucked round the thighs. Dark brown suede jacket open at the front. One arm outflung, the other resting on the breast of a beige sweater. A white face with staring eyes.

In the frozen instant of gazing at the left arm across the breast Stella noticed there was no wedding ring although a gold watch gleamed against a pallid wrist.

A movement distracted her. It was a spider scuttling up a puffy cheek. The spider paused when it reached a glazed eyeball; then it crossed the eyeball and disappeared into a tangle of long dark hair.

The shock of what she saw was never to be forgotten and it was during this numb moment of horror, on the afternoon of April the twenty-eighth, that her peace of mind was shaken to its foundations. She suppressed an almost overwhelming desire to scream and turned to where Rodney was standing holding Max by the collar. Controlling a shake in her voice she said, 'We must report this. Find a phone. Call the police.'

'Call the police,' he said incredulously. 'Whatever for? She's dead. We can't resurrect her.'

In the minor areas of incompatibility which appear on the maps of all intimate relationships the region of law and order was clearly marked on theirs. She, the daughter of a solicitor, was the one who respected the law and 'doing the right thing'. He considered there were two sorts of laws; the laws which suited him and

13

the laws which didn't, and the right course was to adopt what suited self-interest. Once in an argument he had said, 'I don't go along with your naive acceptance of rules you've had no part in making.'

'Call the police,' he repeated, 'all we'd get for doing that would be hassle and aggravation.'

'Hassle! That's all you ever say when you want an excuse to run away.'

They stood facing each other, glowering.

'Are you calling me a coward,' he asked angrily.

'No, but I am saying you dodge issues which cause you personal inconvenience unless, of course, it's part of your job.'

'I'm paid for my job. I'm not paid for finding dead bodies.'

She felt her mouth begin to tremble and fought to keep from either breaking down and crying or flying into a blind rage. 'If you aren't willing to report it,' she said, 'I shall.' She turned on her heel and began to make her way back to the car.

'All right,' he called out grudgingly, 'we'll report it but don't blame me if one day you wish you'd left well alone.'

TWO

They drove to the nearest house, asked to use the phone, and Rodney called the police. When the operator asked him to repeat the number he was calling from he rolled his eyes meaningly at Stella as if to say, 'I told you there'd be hassle.' Then he had difficulty in describing the exact location where the body had been found. Finally he said, 'Santer's Wood? Is that what it's called? Right. We'll go straight back and wait for your men.'

He rang off. 'It's going to be a long day,' he sighed.

Morbid news travels fast and by the time a pair of policemen arrived in a panda-car five curious onlookers had gathered. One policeman said, 'You lead the way, sir,' while the other addressed the small knot of bystanders with the words, 'Everybody keep back.'

More police cars arrived, lights flashing, sirens wailing. Soon the thicket where the dead woman's body lay had been roped off.

A sergeant said, 'Would you and your wife care to follow us in your car. We shall need to take a statement.'

Before replying Rodney looked hard and long at Stella. 'Certainly, sergeant,' he said. 'Always pleased to do my public duty.'

They went to a police station four miles away and Rodney dictated a statement which was typed by a policewoman. After signing it he said to the sergeant, 'I suppose you haven't found out the woman's identity yet?'

'Not yet, sir. But we shall. We shall.'

Rodney turned to Stella, 'Come along, darling, or it'll be time to give Max another walk and he's found enough for one day.'

The sergeant gave a braying laugh as though a joke had been cracked but Stella looked less than amused.

As they walked out of the police station a tousle-haired man in duffle-coat and jeans approached. 'Local Press,' he said, 'I understand you found a body, sir.'

'No comment,' replied Rodney.

'Just a short question . . .'

'No questions. No interview. Good day.'

'You were rather abrupt with that chap,' said Stella as he drove away.

'Was I? Good.'

They hardly spoke again during the rest of the journey.

That evening they received a number of calls from the Press. Eventually Rodney took the phone off its rest.

Most newspapers the following morning carried brief reports on the discovery of a woman's body. Some tried to titillate curiosity by referring to her as an attractive divorcee who had adopted the surname of the man with whom she had been living. Deirdre Jameson, thirty, was variously described as 'live-in companion', 'close friend' and 'housekeeper' to William Jameson, single, fifty, of an address in Ipswich, Suffolk. The police were treating the case as a murder enquiry and were anxious to interview an American serviceman who was seen trying to hitch a lift in the vicinity of Santer's Wood on the afternoon of Thursday, 25 April. The body had been discovered by chance by a Mr and Mrs Rodney Best while walking their dog. They had reported their find to the police immediately.

Before he left home for the conference in Romford Rodney said, 'I doubt if you'll get many calls today. We were news last night but things will have moved on.'

16

She gave a weary smile. 'I'd no idea we'd be so in the limelight.'

'And Max. They wanted his photo.'

'I still think we did the right thing.'

He put an arm round her shoulder and kissed her cheek. 'Of course we did. Just don't stand any nonsense. Put on your stand-no-nonsense-school-teacher-manner.'

'I will. Don't worry. Have a nice day.'

When he returned in the evening the first question he asked was, 'Any harassment?'

'None. Not a thing. The only call was from Marjorie who'd read about it. Oh yes, and Helen.'

He looked relieved. 'Just as I thought.' Then he went to get his usual homecoming drink. The first drink of the evening had a special importance; it signified that he was his own man again and not an employee of Susan's Starters.

As he was pouring a measure of gin Stella said, 'I rang Dad.'

He swung round, almost spilling the drink. 'What did he say?'

'I didn't speak to him. He was in court. He didn't ring back.'

Rodney seemed to relax. 'I expect he'll have read about it in the papers . . . Would you like one?'

'Then I'm surprised he hasn't called back . . . Yes, please.'

He reached for a bottle of tonic water. 'It'll be a nine-day wonder. Hopefully we're out of it now.'

But at seven in the evening, just as Stella was preparing to serve up a meal, the doorbell rang. Rodney answered it and she heard him say, 'Not at all. Come in.' He called out, 'We've got visitors, Stel.'

He had shown two men into the sitting room. One was tough-looking and in his forties, the other was younger,

17

a lantern-jawed fellow who looked as though he had been born and brought up in a funeral parlour. Both wore pale blue shirts, dark blue ties and nondescript suits.

The older man introduced himself. 'Detective Inspector Cook. And this is Sergeant Pinkney.'

With a politeness usually reserved for senior company executives Rodney said, 'Won't you sit down, gentlemen. Can I get you a drink?'

Cook answered. 'No, thank you.' He looked at Stella. 'I hope we haven't come at an inconvenient time.'

She gave a false smile. 'It's all right.'

'We won't detain you long. It's your statement, sir. Just double-checking.'

Cook went through the statement line by line. At one point he paused to look at the dog asleep in front of a brick fireplace in which an empty hearth was partly concealed by an earthenware jar full of tulips.

'I assume that is the dog which caused you to interrupt your journey. Fine dogs, labs. Second only to Allys in my estimation.' For a moment Cook's on-duty poise slipped and he gazed at Max with a sort of fondly parental look. Then he continued reading the statement aloud, pausing at the end of each sentence to see if Rodney wished to add anything.

At the end he said, 'The only thing missed out worth including is something to the effect that Mrs Best, although adjacent when you discovered the deceased, didn't witness the actual moment of discovery.'

Rodney asked if this was important.

Cook gave a thin smile. 'Let us put it this way. Nothing, however trivial it may seem, is unimportant in a murder enquiry.'

Rodney turned to Stella. 'I can't remember, darling. When Max found the body you were right behind me, weren't you?'

She shook her head. 'I was a little way back. I'd just

18

ducked under the branch of a tree when I saw you holding Max's collar. You were crouching forward. I asked what you were doing and you said I mustn't look. It was a body.'

'That's right,' said Rodney. 'I said, it's a body. Max sniffed it out.'

Stella opened her mouth to say something but closed it without uttering a word.

'Fair enough,' said Cook. 'If you wouldn't mind adding a couple of sentences to that effect at the foot of the statement, and then sign, that should about wrap it up and we'll leave you good people to get on with what I have my suspicions is something very tasty in the pot.'

As Rodney wrote Stella saw a look pass between the two policemen. Cook's features remained impassive but a fleeting satisfaction passed across the younger man's face as if he were a pall-bearer who had just discharged a particularly heavy load.

Cook took the statement, folded it and slipped it into a manilla envelope. 'One other point. As you may know, we are anxious to interview anyone who was near the spot on Thursday afternoon. You went up to your cottage on the following evening?'

'That's right.'

'I assume you didn't notice anything unusual as you passed by?'

'I don't even remember passing the place,' said Rodney. 'Now I come to think of it, we went by a different route on the way up. We vary our journeys to the cottage.' He hesitated. 'If I may ask, how do you know the crime was committed on Thursday afternoon?'

'It's virtually certain. The deceased was wearing a wrist-watch. It had stopped at exactly three-fifteen and the date slot showed twenty-five.' Cook turned to Sergeant Pinkney. 'Nothing else, is there?'

'The chocolate wrapper?'

'Ah, yes. I don't suppose, sir, you noticed a

19

screwed-up wrapper from a Mars bar a few feet from the deceased?'

'No, I can't say I did.'

'You hadn't been eating a Mars just before you found the body?'

'No. I'm not a chocolate man. My vices are tobacco and' – he lifted a gin and tonic – 'alcohol.'

'And obviously you didn't see the handbag some yards away, otherwise you would have mentioned it.'

Rodney shook his head.

Cook stood up. 'That's it then. We'll be on our way.'

'How's the enquiry going?' Rodney asked.

'It's proceeding according to plan.'

'No immediate arrests expected?'

'Not immediate, sir.'

The policemen moved unhurriedly to the door, their presences somehow occupying more space than the physical matter of bodies and clothes.

Then Cook paused. 'I assume neither of you had met or seen the deceased before the fateful day?'

'Right,' said Rodney.

'That's right,' said Stella.

'Well, thank you again for your help,' said Cook, casting a last glance at Max.

Rodney showed them out of the house. On his return he said, 'We didn't learn much from that.' It sounded like a complaint.

'What did you expect to learn?'

'I don't know. But they might have been a bit more forthcoming. "Proceeding according to plan" is code for "Mind your own business".'

'But it isn't really our business, is it? We're small cogs in a big wheel.' She moved towards the kitchen.

'Damn,' he said.

She paused. 'What's the matter?'

'I should have asked when the inquest was likely to be.'

'Why? You won't be needed, will you?'

'I might be. Anyway, I'd like to go. If I can wangle the time off.'

'Are you serious?'

'Of course I am,' he replied irritably. 'Why shouldn't I be?'

She smothered a desire to say, 'But why should you go?' Instead she said quietly, 'No reason. I'll go and dish up.'

He went to the inquest but was not called to the witness box. Detective Inspector Cook gave evidence that the murdered woman was Deirdre Cluny who was living under the name of Jameson and she had been identified by the man she lived with, William Jameson. A pathologist gave evidence that death had been caused by manual strangulation.

Rodney came home in a state which was more excited than when he returned from a day's work.

'There wasn't much said in court but I got an earful in a pub where reporters were talking about the case. Our Deirdre was a bit of a girl. One of the Sundays will be bringing out an exclusive with her divorced husband who lives in the north with their two kids. He got custody but she had access. It seems at one time she did a bit of acting and did a TV commercial but it got blacked by Equity because she wasn't in the union. The chap she lived with is old enough to be her father and they reckon she got bored with him and went on the game for kicks. Well, play with fire and you get burned. She asked for it.'

Stella listened in near disbelief. He sounded glad that she was rumoured to be promiscuous, as if sleeping around justified murder. Usually he laughed at displays of moral rectitude – he had once said '"Live and let live" is my motto' – and she gave him a searching look to make sure he wasn't being ironic.

'She asked for it,' he repeated, 'and she got it.'

Stella had a disturbed night's sleep. Unwanted thoughts and images would steal into her mind and before she could stop herself she was on a treadwheel of doubts and uncertainties and it wasn't easy to stop the wheel by telling herself to be sensible or take a grip – phrases of self-encouragement which had worked well in the past – something was nagging to be brought out into the open.

It was after the summer term had started, and in the unlikely context of a staff meeting, that what she had been suppressing could no longer be stifled. There had been a discussion about a series of petty thefts and one teacher had said, 'I suspect the cleaners. The finger of suspicion definitely points at the cleaners.' The finger of suspicion. It was a cliché, a metaphor in a state of terminal fatigue, but suddenly it became revitalised and she could vividly visualise a rigid finger and it was pointing at Rodney. And so, in the middle of a staff meeting she acknowledged to herself that she suspected her husband of knowing more about the life and death of Deirdre Jameson than he should.

She wanted to hurry home to be alone with her thoughts; it was impossible to concentrate on the meeting which had started on the question of supervising school lunches. When at last she was able to leave she hurried to her car calling 'Can't stop' to a colleague who tried to button-hole her about a PTA agenda.

The school was only ten minutes' drive from her home but as she was already late, and Rodney might be there, she drove to a public park. Here, with engine switched off, she sat gazing at the back of a wooden shelter which was covered with graffiti. She stared blankly at the message *Sharon 4 Vince* daubed in white paint and marshalled the facts.

Rodney had insisted that Max found the body – sniffed it out. But Max's sense of smell had atrophied. He was an

22

old dog who could hardly see, hear or smell. Recently a cat had crossed their path and Max hadn't seen it or picked up its scent. Had Max really found the body? If not, why should Rodney want to pretend he had?

There were other worrying points. On the morning they left the cottage he had been dismayed – it wasn't too strong a word – when he found she had changed her mind about staying on. He had tried to persuade her to stay. Why? And why had he insisted on driving, suggested they took the longer route, said Max needed a walk when, so far as she could see, Max wasn't being restless? He had ignored the lay-by and himself selected the place to stop. He had tried to discourage her from coming with him when he walked Max and had hurried ahead so fast that she nearly lost him.

He hadn't wanted to notify the police. Would he have reported the discovery if she hadn't been present?

Finally, he was developing a morbid interest in what he called 'the case' and quite untypically thought Deirdre Jameson had deserved her fate. He generally referred to her as 'the Jameson woman', but once or twice recently had simply called her 'Deirdre' as if she were not a stranger but someone he had known.

Those were the facts stirred up by the finger of suspicion.

Whenever she had doubts or worries she would think of her father and wonder how he would cope. He was the wisest man she knew. She thought of her father now and could almost hear him say, in his laconic manner, 'In this country a man is innocent until proved guilty. Suspicion isn't proof. Where there is doubt the accused should be given the benefit of the doubt. Never judge by appearances. Memory is treacherous, imagination is mischievous, put the two together and you have a self-deception powerful enough to deceive others.'

I'm being stupid, she thought as she drove away. Neurotic. I must get a grip on myself.

As she turned into the driveway of their house she saw his red Ford Granada had been left on the concrete run-in. Usually he put it away in the garage. Why was it outside? Was he going out somewhere?

THREE

'You're late,' he said as she walked in. It wasn't a
reproof. He gave a cheerful smile and lightly pecked her
cheek.

'Staff meeting. It dragged on and on.'

'And I was early. Thought we might go out and
celebrate tonight.'

'Oh? What are we celebrating?'

He stroked his chin thoughtfully and she caught the
faint scent of after-shave lotion.

'Celebrate? Let's see . . . We'll celebrate the birth of
King Ludwig II of Bavaria. Why not?'

'Why not,' she echoed, playing along with the
ridiculous idea so that he wouldn't suspect her of
suspecting something of him.

He grinned with a sort of youthful delight and touched
her shoulder gently with one hand and she remembered
why she had first been physically attracted to him. The
grin had weakened her defences – she had been brought
up to believe that girls and young women needed
'defences' – and his hands, beautifully shaped, elegant
and eloquent, had excited her. And although she was
now far less interested in the sexual side of married life
than he, she could understand that women would find
him attractive.

'Great. I'll ring and book a table for two.'

He walked jauntily to the phone in the hall.

'Think I'll have a bath,' she called after him.

As she turned on the bath taps she remembered something else her father had once said. 'Between the valley of suspicion and the valley of conviction lies a mountain called proof. Has to be scaled. Not enough to take a detour called circumstantial evidence.'

Minutes later, her body enveloped in fragrant water, she thought again of her father. She was an only child and since her mother's death when she was twelve had felt especially close to him. Although she never thought much about the quality of her parents' marriage she sensed that it had been less than ideal and perhaps this was why her father had never remarried. A succession of housekeepers had looked after the home and he had treated them all with a chilly respect accentuated by an abrupt manner. He used the personal pronoun sparingly and this gave his utterances a clipped effect. 'Dislike superfluous verbiage. Can't stick small talk. No good at socialising,' he had once said and it went part of the way towards explaining why he was basically a lonely man and a workaholic.

Nevertheless, with her he was able to relax. When Rodney came on the scene with easy affability and verbal fluency Stella had been afraid her father might treat the younger man with some hostility, even as a rival. She needn't have worried. He did his best to make Rodney welcome, although at times he seemed more like an impeccably civilised diplomat extending hospitality to an emissary from an undeveloped foreign country than a prospective father-in-law.

On his side Rodney realised that an unbridgeable gulf existed and gave up trying to sell himself. 'We shall never be friends,' he said regretfully to Stella after they had married, 'your father's only friends are business friends.'

It had been her dearest wish that the two men who meant most to her should become real friends and when she found she was pregnant she had fantasies of the baby bringing its father and grandfather close together. But the longed-for child was stillborn. The birth had been difficult and she had needed internal stitching and had been warned that due to complications another pregnancy could be fatal. Rodney had promptly undergone a vasectomy and she, putting sorrow behind her, had trained to be a school teacher. If she couldn't have a child of her own she would help in the upbringing of other people's children. Once or twice they had discussed the possibility of adopting a baby but Rodney wasn't in favour of the idea. 'Not yet anyway,' he had said. It was still not yet.

But about two or three years ago (she couldn't put an exact date to it) she had begun to notice a change in the relationship between the two men. It was not possible to give an example of increased familiarity but their handshakes seemed warmer and they appeared more at ease with each other. She hoped very much that Rodney hadn't in some way been involved with Deirdre Jameson, not only for her own peace of mind but because her father had old-fashioned ideas about morality.

She climbed out of the bath and began towelling herself. How would her father react if she told him of her suspicions – not that she would dream of doing so. He would ask, 'Suspicious of what?' Suspicious that Rodney murdered the woman? That he arranged her murder? That he knew she was to be murdered? Suspicious of what precisely?

And she would reply, 'I don't think he murdered her. Rodney isn't that sort of man. But although I'm probably being very silly I can't help thinking he stopped the car at that particular place and for some reason needed to find her body.'

The restaurant was bathed in a deep red glow, candles flared and gutted, and the champagne was going to her head.

He reached out for the bottle and topped up her

glass. 'You're looking very beautiful tonight,' he said.
'I'll bet you say that to all your girl friends.'
'Yes, but only on the thirty-first of April.'
She looked at the hand firmly holding the bottle.
Long, tapering fingers, immaculately kept nails. When
she was feeling slightly tipsy the sight of his hands
could still arouse a quiver of desire.
He replaced the bottle in the ice bucket. The wine
waiter, anxious at the self-service, hurried across.
Rodney gave him a friendly but dismissive wave.
'Are you trying to get me drunk?' she asked with a
smile when the waiter had moved away.
'Now would I do a thing like that! That's for crude
operators. Crude I may be, but I'm not operating.'
'Oh.' She feigned disappointment and raised the
glass to her lips. 'And I'd thought you were making a
play for me.'
He grinned. 'Goddammit, I am.'
She tipped back the glass and swallowed. Before they
set out she had made up her mind that, come what
may, she would give him what he wanted tonight. On
no account must he think she was withholding herself
for an undisclosed reason. None of the excuses used
by herself and countless generations of women –
headache, a terribly tiring day, wrong time of the
month, not in the mood, would be trotted out tonight.
It had, after all, been some time since the last time.
'You're looking thoughtful,' he said.
'I do when I'm thinking.'
Their plates had been cleared and they were waiting
for the sweet trolley. He felt in his pocket for a packet of
cigarettes, almost brought the packet out, and then put
it back.
'Interesting thoughts,' he asked, 'or are you back at
the staff meeting?'
'I was thinking about the cottage. It isn't let over half
term. I might go down and check it over – see Mrs

Prentice has been doing her stuff – and if the weather's fine work on the garden. It'll be a jungle by now.'

'Good idea. When is half term?'

'In a fortnight.'

He frowned. 'I'd like to come, but we shall be damn busy just then.'

'No need. You don't mind doing your own cooking.'

The trolley arrived. She chose profiteroles; he opted for green figs. For a few moments they ate in silence. When he spoke it was about the case and she wondered if he had somehow tuned into her thoughts. Had her suspicions been aggravated because of the almost obsessional interest in the aftermath of his discovery?

'I was chatting with Dickie today and he happened to mention the case. Apparently there's been a similar one in the west country. A woman, out for a bit on the side, letting herself get picked up. Found strangled in a disused barn. Sounds like another Deirdre.'

'Is it in the papers? I haven't read it.'

'Dickie read it in a provincial.'

'I wonder why Deirdre Jameson got so much coverage and this one seems to have less.'

He shrugged. 'Don't know. It might be the American angle. The police must have quizzed just about everyone at the Woodbridge air base on account of an American serviceman having been seen.'

She finished the profiteroles and sat back watching him eat a last fig. When did fascination with an aspect of the dark side of human nature, like murder, become a morbid fascination? And was his fascination with the case simply because he had 'discovered' the body and therefore had played a small part or were there more complex origins?

Since he had introduced the subject she was free to pursue it. 'How does anyone know for sure that the woman in the west country, or Deirdre Jameson for that matter, was out for a "bit on the side"?' She spoke the phrase with distaste.

29

'I don't know about the other woman, but with Deirdre it was obvious.'

He had never once said, 'Poor woman' or 'What a dreadful way to die.' She decided to drop the subject.

When coffee arrived he ordered a brandy for himself and asked what she would like. Usually she declined a liqueur but tonight she thought, I must blur the edges.

'I'd like a Drambuie,' she said. 'We must drink a final toast to good King Ludwig of Bavaria.'

On the way home she watched his hands, lean, flexible, taut, on the steering wheel.

Once home, he took Max for a short walk while she prepared for bed.

The lights were on while he undressed. She looked at the ceiling and wondered if he would switch them off when he got into bed. She hoped so. Her responses were less inhibited in darkness. But he preferred visual to tactile sensations and liked the lights left on. Tonight, without saying anything, he deferred to her preference and the lights went out.

What followed was, thanks to darkness, champagne and Drambuie, and his skill, 'really quite nice'. There was only one moment which could have spoiled everything. Early in the foreplay she felt his hands gently caress her neck and encircle it. Before his fingers could have tightened, even if he had wished to tighten them, she took his wrists and lowered his hands. With an effort of will she blotted out thoughts of Deirdre Jameson.

On her way to the cottage at half term Stella took the long route and as she approached Santer's Wood she slowed down and looked out of the car window. There was nothing to show that the police had once combed the area in a massive murder hunt. The place where she and Rodney had taken Max for a walk was simply a densely shaded patch of woodland crowned by summer-green treetops and a blue sky. As a result of the case she had learned that the land was owned by the highway authority and was designated for road widening. One day a motorway would seal the spot where Deirdre had lain. As for the case, it had faded from the media after increasingly brief reports in which the police maintained their investigations were continuing.

As she accelerated away from the wood she realised that she had fallen into Rodney's habit of thinking of the dead woman as Deirdre.

On arrival at the cottage she let Max out of the car and gave him a short walk before going through the cottage opening windows. While she moved around she wondered why the nagging suspicion persisted that Rodney was implicated in a crime. Perhaps it was because his reactions were so different from what she would have expected. Not only had he never shown any sympathy for Deirdre, he had never said anything like, 'I hope they get the killer.' Instead, more than once, he had said, 'I reckon the fellow who did it is going to get away with it,' and he hadn't sounded displeased.

She paused to look out of the bedroom window at an unspoiled view of the common with its fringe of distant pinewoods. Sparrows twittered in a bush below. Nothing moved except a cloud which drifted slowly like a tattered veil across the sun's face. It was a familiar setting but something was missing. It was the same and yet different. And then she realised why it seemed different. The scene had lost its power to soothe.

That night she dreamed of Rodney climbing through the window with blood streaming from his hands. She came awake with her heart pounding. The strident call of a screech owl tore the night apart and for the first time she felt fear at being alone in the isolated cottage. Not alone. Max was downstairs. Thank God for that, she thought. I'll make myself a cup of tea and settle down.

While waiting for the kettle to boil she went round checking that front and back doors were locked and

31

bolted and all windows securely shut. When the tea was made she sat down at the kitchen table and tried to relax and forget the nightmare. The only sounds were the loud tick of a wall clock and Max snoring gently.

Was Rodney asleep now? Was he even in their bed? Maybe not, but she didn't mind if he wasn't sexually dependent on her, provided he didn't let slip some embarrassing revelation. Unexpectedly, after a few extra loud ticks, the clock stopped. She glanced at its dial where the hands had come to rest at exactly a quarter past three. A quarter past three! The time when Deirdre's watch had stopped. If I was superstitious, she thought, I'd imagine someone or something was trying to get to me; the unquiet spirit of a murdered woman.

She poured another cup of tea. Her father would be very sceptical about any paranormal happening – 'It's all in the mind,' he would say dismissively. Then it occurred to her that she and Rodney had seen very little of him recently although usually he was a regular visitor. But his weekends had been occupied by invitations from influential clients and professional colleagues. She recalled that he found the small hours of the morning the worst. He had once said, 'Never make a decision in the small hours. It's the time depression strikes. Any decision made then will almost certainly be a wrong decision.'

Nevertheless, she made a decision. She would try to find out why Deirdre had died and who had killed her. Although she didn't believe she was married to a murderer she felt that while her suspicions persisted she was married to murder.

The decision brought a certain calm. She went upstairs, climbed into bed and instantly fell asleep.

While she slept a belt of rain scurried in from the north and when she drew the curtains the common looked featureless and drab as if intimidated into anonymity by a lowering grey sky. Her decision, so right at three-

32

fifteen in the morning, seemed in the bleak light of a rain-swept day ridiculously naive. How could a school teacher succeed where murder squad detectives had failed? She knew from newspaper reports that headquarters had been set up in a local police station and that exhaustive enquiries had been made in the neighbourhood. Deirdre's live-in man friend and other men had been interviewed but no one had been charged. Frogmen had vainly searched a large pond for a bracelet Deirdre had been wearing when she left home. It was a mystery why this had been taken, even though it was gold and weighted with little charms, when a valuable gold watch on her other wrist hadn't been removed.

It was in mid-morning after she had been out shopping and was reading the daily paper that she saw a headline – *New lead in murder case*:

> Yesterday Detective Superintendent John Vesty leading the enquiry into the murder of Deirdre Jameson, Ipswich divorcee and one-time actress, whose body was found on 28 April, appealed for information from anyone who had seen a red saloon car, make and registration number unknown, parked in the vicinity of Santer's Wood on the afternoon of the previous Thursday. Det. Supt. Vesty said that information could provide a breakthrough and anyone who could remember seeing such a car should contact him immediately.

Stella put the paper down. Without details of make or registration the so-called lead seemed tenuous, but it was disconcerting that Rodney's company car was red. The news item added another skein to a thickening web of suspicion and the decision made in the small hours, but later doubted, was once again given credibility. But this time her angle was different. It wasn't a question of who killed Deirdre Jameson; the problem was to make sure Rodney wasn't involved. The police wanted to find a murderer; she wanted to find her husband innocent.

It was impossible to settle. She picked up a book and put it down, went to wash the curtains, decided against it, and finally cleaned a copper kettle which stood on the stone hearth. She polished until the metal glowed as if fired by some ancient warmth and as she rubbed she remembered how, after reporting the discovery, she had gone back to wait for the police. He had said, 'Not my week. First my wallet, and now this!'

She paused from polishing. She had forgotten about the wallet he had lost two or three days previously. She put down the kettle and unhooked a brass ladle with long iron handle which hung on the wall by the fireplace. As she polished the brass she thought about the wallet.

It had never been found. He had come home very late on Thursday evening looking drained after a long day. The casserole she had kept warm had almost dried up but this didn't matter because he had little appetite.

'We had beer and sandwiches sent up,' he had explained.

Earlier he had phoned her to say he'd be late owing to an extended company meeting.

'Hardly worth changing,' he had said. Usually when he came home he changed into casual gear. 'I'll just take off my jacket.'

It had been as he was draping the jacket over a chair that he exclaimed, 'My God!'

'What's the matter?'

'My wallet. It's gone!'

He had stood, jaw sagging, eyes wide, looking like a small boy who has lost a month's pocket money. Then he made a frantic search of all pockets.

'Perhaps you dropped it in the car,' she had suggested.

'Yes. I'll have a look.'

He had rushed out of the room. When he came back

minutes later he was ashen-faced. 'It's not there. It must have been stolen.'

'Stolen? When?'

'I slipped out of the meeting to buy some cigarettes. I remember being jostled as I came out of the shop. A couple of yobbos. I wasn't wearing an overcoat. I'll bet one picked my pocket while the other got belligerent. Told me to look where I was going.'

'Did you have much in it?'

'Not much money but all my credit cards.'

'What'll you do?'

He had thought. 'No point in reporting it. I couldn't describe the youths. But I'll have to call the credit card people first thing in the morning.'

The colour had slowly returned to his cheeks but he had remained withdrawn, as though he had something on his mind. After a nightcap of whisky he had said, 'I'm tired. I think I'll turn in.'

She hung up the brass antique ladle and put away cleaning materials.

What next? Rain was pattering against the window and the scene outside was drably grey-green and desolate. Max was curled up on the rug and snoring.

She moved aimlessly away from the window and stood in the centre of the room. Something important was teasing the edges of memory. Another triviality which in itself would be meaningless but in aggregate with other trivialities might be an indicator of suspicion justified.

She frowned in an effort of concentration. His wallet. It wasn't in the car. The car! Deirdre had been murdered on that Thursday. The police were appealing for information from anyone who had seen a red saloon in the vicinity of Santer's Wood. Rodney's car was a red saloon. He had come home very late.

She looked at the sleeping dog. 'Come on, Max,' she said. 'I can't stand it here. We're going home.'

FOUR

She had been travelling just over an hour when she saw the loop of road which skirted Santer's Wood. On impulse she slowed down and finally stopped. For a few moments she sat quietly and then, unsure of her own motivations and what she might expect to find, she got out and made her way into the wood. It was easy to find the place where they had discovered Deirdre. Undergrowth had been beaten down and the thicket partly cleared. She looked around at a network of trees. Bushes and brambles gave off a strong odour of damp vegetation. She could hear the hum of traffic on the highway but no birds sang and this was surprising because wildlife should have thrived in the wood.

Out of curiosity she went past the thicket into an unknown part of the wood. Very soon she reached its perimeter and was looking across an arable field bordered by hawthorn hedge. A five-barred gate in the hedge showed there might be a lane close by.

After a few moments she made her way back to the car. The diversion had provided no insights or proofs but she felt she had taken the first positive step in her quest for answers to the questions which swarmed in her mind.

Although she had been away only one night, instead of the planned three, the house had a peculiarly sterile atmosphere. She knew at once that Rodney hadn't spent last night at home. Everything was exactly as she had left it; no cigarette butts in ashtrays, no dishes in the sink, all windows securely shut, no record sleeve dropped carelessly on the floor and no lingering smell of stale cigarette smoke.

After taking her overnight bag to the bedroom and giving Max some biscuits and a drink of water she went to the room Rodney used as a study. It was here, when he had been a junior rep selling the products of Susan's Starters, that he would laboriously enter his daily returns. It was a small room furnished with desk, side table, bookshelves and a music centre. Wall space was filled with a poster showing Marilyn Monroe holding down her dress as she stood on a hot air grille, a Pirelli calendar for the previous year, and three framed photographs of a school football team.

She knew that in a deep drawer in the side table buried under a litter of company papers was a box-file filled with Press cuttings. Although it was no secret that the key to this and other drawers were kept in a pewter beer-mug she felt a slight sense of shame as she reached into the mug. After rifling through a compost of papers she pulled out the box-file. Sitting in a swivel chair by the desk she read carefully through each cutting.

Deirdre Jameson had married at the age of eighteen. She had two children by her husband, Neil Pensom, who ran a small general store. After their divorce he had been awarded custody of the children although she had limited access and was entitled to maintenance. In the period between divorce and meeting William Jameson she had a number of jobs, including acting, and for a short period her name was linked with the wayward son of an earl. It was clear from various reports that she had never lacked male escorts and it was also obvious that William Jameson had spent many hours helping the police with their enquiries.

Jameson had last seen her at 12.45 on Thursday when she said she was going to see a friend (but had not named the friend) and expected to be back for the evening meal. The first he knew of her death was a call from the police during the evening. Her car had been found in an Ipswich side street and it was presumed she had either been picked up there by someone known to her or had hitched a lift and the driver had taken her to Santer's Wood. Jameson had given a description of the clothes she was wearing and also her jewellery.

Most of the newspaper photographs showed a smiling woman leaning against a garden gate. One paper flatteringly called her 'the Joan Collins of Ipswich'. It was shortly after reading this that Stella came across a plain envelope inside which was a glossy head and shoulders photo of Deirdre Jameson. A heart-shaped face framed by a tumble of dark wavy hair. Arched eyebrows, straight nose, full rather pouting lips. On the reverse of the photo was an indelible stamp showing that the copyright belonged to the Viva Model Agency.

Beneath the photo was a cutting of an exclusive interview with Neil Pensom who, if he knew the maxim *de mortuis nil nisi bonum*, ignored it, although he admitted she'd had a poor start in life as a casualty of a broken home. Her father had been an Irish labourer employed on road construction; her mother, a school-mistress, was English and middle-class. Stella's interest quickened. Deirdre's mother, like her, had been a school teacher.

She continued reading. According to Neil Pensom, Deirdre had been very fond of her father who told her stories from Irish mythology. But when she was seven her parents were divorced and her father returned to Ireland where he was killed trying to stop a runaway horse. She was brought up by her mother, a disciplinarian who found fault with everything she did but who was 'a number one hypocrite because she was no better than she should be'.

After making this enigmatic comment Pensom went on to say, 'From the time the honeymoon ended it was

38

nothing but quarrels. She refused to help in the shop even though she'd agreed to before we were wed. The only good times were in bed and that was spoiled when I found out she'd been sleeping with my best friend's father. That really got my goat. She sneered at my friend, called him a moron, but she fancied his father who was a boozer and had a minus I.Q. We had a hell of a row and she told me he wasn't the first. She really provoked me but I kept my cool. It doesn't surprise me in the least she has ended up the way she has. Sooner or later she was bound to meet someone who couldn't keep his rag. In a way I'm sorry for her, of course, but don't forget I was still having to pay maintenance while she had what must have been a fairly easy number as housekeeper to someone much better off than me.'

There was more of much the same stuff, some of it dangerously close to being libellous. The article ended with the information that he was happily remarried and now lived in Newcastle.

Stella put down the cutting. Presumably the police had interviewed Neil Pensom and eliminated him from any list of suspects. There were more cuttings, none of which added to Stella's knowledge of the dead woman or threw light on who might have killed her. Finally, at the bottom of the box-file, was a photocopy of an article in *The Criminologist* in which a forensic scientist wrote about homicide victims who had died from manual strangulation.

She placed the papers carefully back in the box-file and snapped it shut. Then she glanced through the company papers. Mostly these concerned sales targets, management objectives, statistical evaluations, and so on, but her attention was caught by a memorandum on advertising.

It is to be regretted that Viva Model Agency saw fit to supply an actress who had not been given Union

39

clearance and, as a result, the commercial had to be filmed with a different actress. However, doubts exist as to whether Viva was appraised of the possible difficulties of employing a non-union actress and in these circumstances our legal department advises that no action should be taken against the agency. The whole exercise has proved more costly than initial projections and the Board is not convinced that television advertising is the best way to promote our very wide range of products. Accordingly in future the financial allocation for advertising will not include any expenditure on television commercials.

Stella closed and locked the drawer. She remembered that Rodney had visited a studio where a commercial was being made for water chestnut soup, a new line for Susan's Starters, and she had a vague recollection that he had mentioned some snag connected with industrial relations. He had seemed unconcerned, and she had forgotten the incident. But now she realised he must have met Deirdre at the studio. If so, was it a chance and only meeting, or had there been other meetings?

She had always thought that Rodney, with his dislike of hassle, would never commit himself to an affair. If he was anything he was a brief encounter man, and the briefer the better. Now she wasn't so sure.

When he hadn't returned home by eleven she decided to go to bed but, out of curiosity, before turning in she went to a drawer where he kept a leather case containing spare razor, toothbrush and other items needed when he had to stay somewhere overnight. The case wasn't in the drawer.

On the following morning she phoned his office and spoke to his assistant, a girl called Jill whom she'd met at company dinners.

'He's had to go to Birmingham,' said Jill. 'He's got to

sort out a dreadful overstocking of paté.'
'I was calling to let him know I've come back early from the cottage.'
Was it her imagination or did Jill's voice change slightly, become more guarded.
'I can get a message through to him if you like.'
'No. Don't worry. But if he comes back today tell him I called . . . By the way, Jill, do you have his diary there?'
A silence followed by a grudging, 'I can get it.'
'It's simply to check a date, if it's not too much trouble. I've got a friend here and we've just had an argument about when she and her husband last saw us. I'm sure it was Wednesday, April the twenty-fourth. She swears it was Thursday, the twenty-fifth. But I'm sure Rodney was working late that night at a conference.'
'If you'll hold on, I'll have a look.'
As she waited Stella thought, That was stupid of me. I wouldn't be calling to let Rodney know I was back if I had a friend here. Would I? No. I'd wait until I was alone.
'Hello . . . I've got it. The conference for that Thursday was cancelled.'
'Thanks, Jill. I must have got it wrong.'
So the story of being kept late at the conference was a lie and so was the story that he'd had his wallet stolen when he'd slipped out to buy cigarettes.

She heard his car pull up, the door slam and moments later his key in the door. She hurried into the sitting room, picked up a magazine and began reading.
'Anyone at home?' he called.
'I'm in here.'
It had been a warm day. He was in shirt sleeves, jacket slung over his shoulders. His face was flushed.
'I got your message. Jill contacted me.' He dropped

41

the jacket on a chair and went to the drinks cabinet. 'Can I get you one?'

'A Martini. With ice, please.'

As he was getting the drinks, and without looking at her, he asked, 'What on earth was all that about a bet?'

'A bet?'

'Jill said you'd got a bet with a friend about when she last saw us.'

Stella laughed. 'It wasn't a bet. Linda was here for coffee and we had an argument about when they'd last come round for dinner. There wasn't a bet. Anyway, it was only incidental. The main thing was to let you know I was home.'

He took his time pouring the drinks. As he handed over hers he said, as if there had been no intervening silence, 'And it's nice to have you home, but you don't usually phone when you get back.'

'I got back yesterday afternoon.'

The muscles in his face tightened. 'I see.' He moved the jacket, let it drop on the carpet, and sat down. With a studied movement he placed a long glass of gin and tonic on a side table, judging exactly the spot where it would be most convenient. The manoeuvre enabled him to begin speaking without looking at her.

'I spent the night at the Simpsons. When Jack heard I was on my Jack Jones . . . Jack – Jack Jones – there should be a joke in that somewhere, never mind . . . he invited me round for the evening. Betty had already got other people coming. It was quite a party. Jack's always very liberal with the booze. They convinced me I shouldn't drive and offered me a bed.'

She could have said she knew he'd been away more than one night and asked where he'd been on the second night, not with Jack Simpson twice running, surely. But all she said was, 'That was very nice of them.'

'Yes.'

He shot her a quick glance, head slightly tilted to one side. It was a movement she recognised and signified he was trying to assess her mood. A faint sigh and a fractional relaxation of his body indicated that he had assessed her mood, wrongly, as benign, but she didn't intend to disillusion him. It was important that he shouldn't be suspicious of her enquiry about dates or his whereabouts on two previous evenings.

'Are we eating in tonight?' he asked.

'What would you like? Something cold with salad?'

'Sounds good. It was hellish hot in town.'

'A cold consommé to start with?'

He rolled his eyes in mock horror. Years of sales promotions and innumerable tastings had numbed his appetite for soup.

She laughed. 'All right, we'll have mackerel.'

'And after we've eaten I'll cut the grass. I meant to do it the night before last but it rained.'

You weren't here the night before last, she thought. She said, 'It rained at the cottage, too.'

'Is that why you came home early? Bad weather?'

Telling lies only troubled him if he thought they might be nailed. He had once admitted that his instinctive reaction to an awkward question, before he had time to think, was to lie. She was different. Her initial response was always to tell the truth. His question was awkward but she wanted to avoid telling a lie. Rather slowly she said, 'It was partly the weather. Partly I just wanted to get home. I didn't sleep well.'

'Something on your mind?'

'Plenty. You know me. If it's not one thing, it's something else.'

He nodded. 'I'll bet it's to do with the school. You're too conscientious. I've told you that a thousand times. You should be like me. Take each day as it comes, forget yesterday and don't worry about tomorrow.'

'I sometimes wish I could.'

43

The trace of sadness in her voice was lost on him. 'When are we eating then?' he asked.

Late that evening he went to put away the car and, although it was still warm outside, he put on his jacket. When he returned she noticed a slight bulge at the waist-line. He hurried upstairs and she guessed he was putting his toilet case back in a drawer in the bathroom.

She didn't like the idea that he might have spent the past two nights with another woman, but a passing infidelity was nothing more than a pale shadow compared to the red stain of murder. She was glad that he didn't try to initiate love-making when they retired for the night but switched off the light and said, 'It's been a long day. I should sleep like a log.'

Within minutes he was breathing heavily, but she lay awake examining yet again all the straws which bonded into a sheaf of suspicion.

Breakfast. He was eating cereal with a newspaper propped in front of him.

'I see Detective Superintendent John Vesty is in charge of another murder case. Body of a man found in an attic in Birmingham. Funny, I was there only yesterday.' He laughed. 'I must be a catalyst or something. Murder follows me around.' He pulled a falsely anxious face. 'Do you think I'm some sort of *homme fatal?*'

'I've thought you were for some time,' she said and smiled.

'Deirdre's case has been pushed into the background. Other cases are coming along.' There was a note of satisfaction in his voice.

'Talking of Deirdre,' she said, 'wasn't there something about her doing a TV commercial? I wonder what it was.'

He became very interested in the contents of his

cereal bowl. 'I've no idea.'

'But the commercial was never shown because she wasn't a member of Equity. Didn't you have some trouble with something like that a few years ago?'

He looked up, his face a defensive blank. 'Did I? Oh, yes. That was Birmingham too. Odd how Birmingham keeps cropping up.'

'Even odder if it was Deirdre in the commercial for Susan's Starters.'

'It would be,' he replied coolly. 'But I was only around to make sure they didn't muck around with the colouring. The advertising agency wanted some chemical additive put in to make it look more appetising but our Board was dead against it. I got landed with the job of making sure the genuine stuff was used. In the end the colour was all right but the actress was all wrong, whoever she was. Can't say I remember the Jameson woman being around.'

FIVE

Stella didn't like being called houseproud. The word was applied exclusively to women (men were never houseproud, nor were they car-proud or job-proud) and it seemed to her that 'houseproud' was a sort of consolation prize awarded in the absence of any other merit, rather like a prize for the neatest kept desk awarded to a dull pupil. Even so, she was, in the best sense, houseproud. She took pride in keeping appliances and furnishings spotless, sills and ledges dusted, carpets vacuumed, and wood, copper and brass polished. A daily chore was to check the bathroom because although Rodney did his best to leave it clean after shaving and showering he usually missed some splash marks.

It was as she was leaving the bathroom she paused by a small cabinet and on impulse opened a drawer. Rodney's toilet-case was back in place. She had been right in thinking the bulge under his jacket was the smuggled case. It was a pity he liked to smuggle, to deceive. But smuggling of any sort appealed to him. They never took a holiday abroad without him smuggling something, frequently of no great value, through Customs. He got a kick from going through undetected; it was a kick she didn't share.

Almost without thinking she picked up the case and pulled its zip-fastener. Inside, held by leather loops, were three stainless steel containers. A long one for toothbrush; the shorter ones for shaving brush and

46

shaving stick. But Rodney never used a shaving stick, preferring lather from a tube, and this container had never been used except when he smuggled in a gold watch from Tangier. A small safety razor in plastic box, steel mirror and nail scissors, completed the contents.

Later she couldn't remember why she took out the shaving stick container. It may have been the memory of the smuggled watch and a curiosity to see whether he had again been going through Customs when he walked in from the garage last night. The container was surprisingly heavy. She shook it. A metallic rattle within.

Aware that her heart was beating fast she began unscrewing the cap. Then she paused, ashamed. It had been different with the box-file; he had made no secret of that; but now she was prying. Another twist of the container cap and something slid out of the steel tube, slipped through her fingers and fell to the floor.

It was a glittering gold bracelet on to which tiny charms were fastened. She stooped and picked it up as though it were a coiled snake. For some minutes she gazed at it, examining each charm. Among others were a witch on a broomstick, a replica of Big Ben, St Christopher, a scorpion, a pair of dice, a boot with a high heel, an elephant, a skull, a canoe, crossed swords and a portcullis. She had no doubt it was the bracelet which had belonged to Deirdre Jameson. It would be stretching coincidence to infinity to believe there was a rational explanation for the concealed bracelet which didn't involve Deirdre.

She put the bracelet back in the tube, screwed the top, placed the tube in the case, zipped up the case, and put the case in the drawer. It was as she closed the cabinet that a speck of gold caught her eye. A charm which had become detached was lying on the bathroom floor. She stooped and picked it up. It was a little long-eared, one-legged Lincoln Imp. She hesitated, uncer-

47

tain whether to put it back with the bracelet. Then she closed her fist over it and hurried to the bedroom where, after wrapping it in tissue, she popped it into a used lipstick container in her handbag. It wasn't theft, she told herself; she didn't intend to keep the charm permanently but it was tangible evidence with which to confront Rodney if she needed to have a showdown.

She went to the garage, got out her car and within twenty minutes was in a village some twelve miles from her home. She found a public call box and dialled the number which had been given in a newspaper as the number on which to contact the police with information concerning the death of Deirdre Jameson.

She asked to be put through to Detective Superintendent Vesty. A delay. She was asked for her name and address. She refused to give it and was then asked what exactly did she want to tell the superintendent.

She guessed efforts might be made to trace her call and said, 'Unless I speak to someone who knows all about the case involving the murder of Deirdre Jameson I shall ring off.'

She was put through to a man who said rather wearily, 'Detective Inspector Cook here. Can I help you?'

She nearly panicked. Would he recognise her voice? Raising the pitch and trying to mimic a north country accent she said, 'I just wanted to know what charms were on the bracelet Deirdre Jameson was wearing.'

'Why? Have you found a bracelet, madam?' Cook's voice was suddenly crisp.

'What were the charms? I'm ringing off if you won't tell.'

'Let me see . . .'

'I'm ringing off.'

'Just a moment. I've a list here. Let me see.'

'Good-bye, mister . . .'

48

'Hold it! An elephant, a clock tower, what looks like a mask–it could be a skull–a witch riding a broomstick . . .'

She replaced the receiver while he was in mid-sentence and hurried from the phone box, keeping her head down. As she drove away from the village she decided the time had come to face Rodney and demand an explanation.

Choosing the right moment is the key to successful confrontation and Stella had thought the right moment might be while he was unwinding with a pre-prandial drink. She was put off balance by a whirlwind entry and a big hug and kiss.

'Get changed, my lovely. Tonight we dine in style after we've done a show.' He dipped into his pocket and from a new pigskin wallet produced theatre tickets for a West End musical. 'How, you may ask, did I get these when the show's booked solid till Christmas? Money plus influence is the answer.'

He was elated, grin at its widest, eyes crinkling.

She said, 'What's happened?'

'I spent the afternoon with the chief buyer for the Superfood chain, just about the biggest chain in the south and east and got him to agree to stock our entire range of starters under our own label, not theirs, with special displays at certain key stores. That's all. Nothing much really. But you may well be looking at a director designate.'

'That's terrific.'

He released her from a breath-taking embrace. 'When the deal was clinched we had a celebratory drink and I felt the sort of power kick a tycoon must get . . . Well, a mini-tycoon.'

She turned her head away so that he wouldn't see the look in her eyes and sense her fierce desire to cut his triumph to ribbons. She had only to say, 'You are a liar,

49

probably a thief and possibly a murderer,' to see him transformed from exultant hero to stunned nonentity.

He realised that something wasn't quite right. Perhaps she couldn't quite grasp the enormity of his achievement. 'What is it, darling?'

She turned her head and looked him full in the face. 'Nothing. It's marvellous news. I'm so glad for you.'

'It's for you, too. For us.' He glanced at his watch. 'Come on. We haven't got a lot of time.'

'Right. I'll go and get ready.'

'I'll fix the drinks,' he called after her. 'This beats King Ludwig of Bavaria, doesn't it?'

It was one of the worst evenings of her life. It was impossible to erase the memory of the gold bracelet, but having decided to go through with the celebration, and not to spoil his treat, she felt like a twenty-four carat hypocrite. It was bad enough at the theatre, enthusing during the intervals, but an ordeal later at a restaurant where the service was slow and he was obviously intent on wooing her.

On the way home, caught up in late night traffic in the tawdry glitter of Shaftesbury Avenue, he asked, 'You did enjoy it, didn't you?'

'Yes, of course. Why?'

'I don't know. You seemed a bit distant once or twice. As if you weren't exactly in the here and now.'

This was it, an opportunity to bring into the open what was troubling her but as she opened her mouth he had to brake suddenly to avoid a weaving jay-walker. She closed her mouth. He would need all his concentration to drive safely.

But on the journey she spoke as little as possible; if nothing else he should get the message that she wasn't in the mood for love-making.

It was when they were home and she had made herself a cup of tea and he had a glass of brandy in his hand, and they were sitting in armchairs, that he asked rather tentatively if she had a headache.

'No, I haven't got a headache.'

'You seem to have gone very quiet. Is something wrong?'

She braced herself. This was the showdown. 'Yes. There is something wrong.'

He withdrew into the recess of his chair in the way a mollusc, sensing danger, retreats into its shell. 'Go on,' he said.

'I've been worried sick for some time. I've suspected you of untruths and downright lies, but today it was something worse. I found the charm bracelet. It was Deirdre's, wasn't it?'

He tossed off the brandy and jumped up to get another.

'Well,' she asked.

'Just a minute.'

Firmly-reined self-control broke under the strain of his 'Just a minute.'

'Just a minute nothing! I want an answer.'

His hand trembled as he held the bottle. A few drops fell on the carpet. 'Sorry,' he muttered out of habit. It was the apology of a husband conditioned by living with a houseproud wife.

'Answer me!'

He took a deep breath, as if psyching himself, and said, 'What were you doing nosing around in my belongings?'

'I'll tell you what. I saw you sneak in last night. I know you didn't stay at the Simpsons on the spur of the moment. You wouldn't have had your shaving kit with you. And anyway, you were away two nights, not one as you made out.'

'I see. And that justified you in nosing through my belongings, did it?'

He took a swig of brandy and put down the glass.

They were standing in the middle of the room facing each other like duellists.

She thrust. 'So the mini-tycoon thinks attack is the best method of defence. Accuse me of nosing so you can get out of answering straight questions. What were you doing with Deirdre's bracelet? Did you take it when we gave Max a walk? Like a common thief. Or had you taken it earlier? Don't tell me she gave it to you. "Here you are, darling, take my bracelet as a keepsake."'

'And what makes you think it belonged to her?' he parried. 'Communication from beyond the grave?'

'No. Communication with the police.'

She was viciously pleased to see his jaw sag. That would teach him not to ask stupid, caustic questions.

'The police?'

His dismay was like the shot of a stimulant drug to her.

'Yes. The police.' She spelled it out. 'P-O-L-I-C-E.'

If he had been a duellist he would have dropped his foil. It was now a different sort of contest. He shook his head. 'What a bloody silly thing to do,' he said, not aggressively, but quietly like a senior master chastening a junior for immaturity.

This change of attitude, which she interpreted as condescending, infuriated her to the point where she wanted to hurt at all costs. She was still duelling and she aimed a thrust well below the belt. 'It was Detective Inspector Cook as a matter of fact. I phoned and made sure he didn't recognise my voice. He confirmed from my description that the bracelet was Deirdre's. I rang off before he had a chance to trace the call . . . I should think he's a good detective. Virile. Positive.' She looked him up and down. 'A real man!'

'What do you mean by that?'

'Work it out for yourself.'

In a voice thick with emotional pain he said, 'The vasectomy was for your sake, not mine.'

She was horrified. 'I didn't mean that. I didn't mean that at all.'

'Whether you meant it or not, you've obviously got a burning grievance. Let's have it.' He forced a smile. 'Let's have it from the top, as they say.'

She went to her chair, feeling drained. She had drawn blood and the sight had numbed her. 'All right,' she said in a voice as quiet as his. 'From the top. I've been unsettled from the moment you found the body. Or did you find it? That's what I've wondered. Perhaps you knew already it was there. And then all those Press cuttings. That was untypical.'

She paused, waiting for a reply.

'I was interested in the case. It was something I'd started by finding a body. Or, to be accurate, Max and I started.'

'On the Thursday when Deirdre was killed you told me you'd been kept late at a conference.'

He gave a sigh. 'I get it. That's why you phoned Jill. Checking up on me. You accuse me of lies and dishonesty but snooping in my belongings and making sneaky phone calls strikes me as being pretty underhand.'

'Where were you on that Thursday?'

'What's this? An interrogation on behalf of your virile friend, Inspector Cook?'

'Now you're being silly. Where were you?'

'That isn't your business.'

'Yes it is. I happen to be married to you and I'm entitled to ask where you were that Thursday.'

'You can ask but the only answer you'll get is that I was helping a friend.'

'What help? What friend?'

He picked up the brandy glass, found it empty, and put it down again.

'All right then,' she said, 'I'm left to draw my own conclusions.'

'You can draw water, draw breath, draw on a bloody school blackboard for all I care. Draw away. Look, it's been a long day. Up till now it's been a good day. The best of my career. But you've completely ruined it, and I'm tired. We'll talk about this in the morning.'

'No. I want to have it out tonight. You won't tell me where you were on Thursday, you behave out of character on the Sunday, you tell me lies about where you stayed last night, and you hid Deirdre's bracelet – the bracelet she was wearing when she was last seen alive. How do you think I feel?'

'Lousy, I expect. And so do I. And I'm going to bed.'

As he moved towards the door she jumped up and stood in his way.

'A red saloon car was seen parked by Santer's Wood on the Thursday.'

He raised his eyebrows wearily. 'So what?'

'Your car is red.'

The weariness left him. 'So that's it! You think I killed her. You really think I'm a murderer.'

'I don't know what to think when you're so evasive.'

'Christ Almighty! Do you think if I had, I'd have let you see how interested I was in the case? I didn't make any secret about collecting clippings from the papers. If I'd . . .' For a moment he was lost for words. 'If I'd done anything like that I'd have made bloody sure I was indifferent. I'd act as if the whole thing bored me. I certainly wouldn't have talked about it the way I have.'

'I admit that's the one thing . . .' It was her turn to be lost for words.

'Don't let any doubts cross your mind,' he said bitterly. 'You've already convicted me of murder. You'd better run and tell your pal, Cook.' He pushed past her. 'Good night.' At the door he paused. 'I'll spare you the horror of sleeping with a murderer. I'll use the other room.'

The door slammed shut after him. Tears came to her

eyes and ran down her cheeks as silently she cried.

At three in the morning she tip-toed into the darkened bedroom where he lay.

'Are you awake?' she whispered.

It took him a long time to reply. 'Yes.'

She came forward and perched on the end of the bed. 'Please, please tell me. If the two nights you spent away were spent with another woman I can't pretend I'd like it, but I'd understand. I wouldn't hold it against you.'

From the darkness he said, 'Thanks very much.' It was spoken with cutting sarcasm.

'So let's forget about those nights. I won't mention them again. But please tell me where you were on that Thursday.'

He was silent.

'I've been thinking,' she said. 'Maybe some of my conclusions were wrong but you don't know what agonies of mind I've been through. But even if the worst was true I wouldn't rat on you. It wasn't fair to suggest I'd go running to Cook.'

He remained silent but she had the feeling it was the silence of indecision rather than refusal. She wished she could see his face. 'Can we have the light on?' she asked, almost timidly.

His reply was almost inaudible. 'Thought you liked bedrooms kept dark.'

Her heart leapt. It was as if the barrier between them was beginning to crumble. And her own response, that of hope rising, astonished her because she realised that, contrary to everything she had thought during previous weeks, a part of her was still in love with him. She shifted up the bed so that she was closer.

'My eyes are getting adjusted,' she said. 'Perhaps we don't need the light.'

And then she felt his hand as it searched for hers. When found, he grasped her hand firmly.

'I did not–repeat not–kill Deirdre Jameson. If you don't trust me on anything else, you must trust me on that.'

It was still dark in the bedroom but she felt as though it had been flooded by a radiant light.

'I do trust you, but . . .'

'I didn't kill her.'

'But you do know much more about it than I do. More about it than the police do.'

'Just trust me.'

'And you can't tell me more than that?'

'Right.'

'I'm sure you've got good reasons.'

'I think I have.'

She leaned over so that her head was close to his. 'I'm so glad. You don't know what a relief . . .'

And then she was in bed with him and he was holding her tight. If he had initiated love-making she would have responded. But he didn't. He simply held her close and this was what she needed most.

SIX

From that night by mutual consent talk about 'the case' was taboo. But Stella didn't forget Deirdre Jameson and sometimes the thought that nothing had changed would sneak into her mind. Rodney had been involved and his involvement never explained. And there was always the chance that one day, when she was least expecting it, the doorbell would ring and the shape of Detective Inspector Cook, or someone like him, would loom ominously through frosted glass. On opening the door she would be greeted by a grimly polite voice – 'Good morning, Mrs Best, we have reason to believe . . .'

A curious reversal took place. In the past it had been Rodney who had foraged through newspapers for gleanings about the murder enquiry, now it was she who surreptitiously did just this. More than once she went through the papers in the box-file only to find he had added nothing. Although on the surface she had little in common with Deirdre Jameson, except for age, she felt a strange affinity with the dead woman and would gaze at the publicity photo trying to fathom what had lain behind sparkling eyes with thick black lashes.

But she always felt slightly guilty about going into Rodney's study and unlocking the drawer where the box-file was kept and so one Thursday, when she was sure he would be at Romford, she took the papers and made copies on the school photocopier. She now had her own collection of papers and it was unnecessary to go to

57

the study. It didn't occur to her that by carrying on the collection he had started she might be nurturing a morbid interest which could grow into an obsession.

The summer term drew to a close and one of her last jobs was to set a holiday project. With a mixed group of girls and boys, and mindful of the pressures exerted by the PTA committee who had warned that any homework or holiday task which was sexist, racist, ageist or speciesist, would be severely condemned, the range of suitable subjects had shrunk to a dull core of safe topics. In the end she chose wild flowers. 'Write about them. Go out and look. Collect and press. Draw pictures of them. Make a scrapbook all about wild flowers.' And to a boy who protested that the project was a 'bit pansified' she retorted firmly, 'Wild flowers, Bernard, are like you. Unruly, undisciplined flowers. You should have a fellow feeling for them.'

Now that Rodney never mentioned Deirdre, she found she ached to talk about her, and whereas once her heart had sunk when he said, 'I've been thinking about the case and . . .', now she longed to speak these same words. The need to find out more about Deirdre had become a hunger and the project on wild flowers might be a way to satisfy her appetite. She had read about William Jameson's curt refusals to give Press interviews or to be tempted to sell a *My Life With Deirdre* story, but he was an expert on wild flowers and this might gain her access to him.

She decided to write a letter enclosing a stamped addressed envelope for his reply.

Dear Mr Jameson,
May I introduce myself? I am a teacher at a comprehensive school and have care of a class of twelve- and thirteen-year-olds. For a holiday project I have set them the task of producing some-thing about wild flowers – scrapbooks, essays,

albums of pressed flowers, etc.

I had heard of your book on the subject which unfortunately my local bookshop couldn't supply, but I had better luck with the public library. I enjoyed your book immensely and was fascinated to read that you have a garden full of wild flowers.

Would it be asking too much if I ask to pay you a visit? I should love to see your garden and promise I would take up very little of your time. It would be a great help to me when going through the children's completed projects. If you are too busy, I will quite understand.

Again many thanks for the enjoyment your book gave,

> Yours sincerely,

She paused and put down her pen. Before starting the letter she had intended to sign with her maiden name, Mytton, so that he wouldn't associate her surname with the Best who had found Deirdre's body. But although some of the values instilled in childhood, like honesty and doing the right thing, had become less imperative in the past few months she still hesitated about using a pseudonym. The contents of the letter were deceit enough without compounding the deception with a false name.

She picked up the pen and wrote boldly, *Stella Best*.

After sealing the envelope she took Max for a walk to the post-box.

His reply came a few days later.

Dear Mrs Best,

I should be delighted to see you and show you round my garden. As you may have gathered I am a conservationist and anything which will introduce the coming generation to the need to preserve the countryside has my whole-hearted support. Wild flowers have so much to offer, not only their beauty and subtle scents, but also the basis of many remedies for human ailments. Please give me a call at the above number so that we can arrange a suitable date.

Yours sincerely,
William Jameson

Stella felt a surge of triumph as she read the letter. 'Done it, Max,' she said. The flutter of guilt that deceit should be successful was quickly suppressed.

She phoned later in the day. A thin, rather tired voice said, 'Yes?'

'This is Stella Best. You kindly said I could visit you.'

The voice took on a more resonant timbre. 'Ah, I'm glad you called. I'm going away for a few days shortly. If you'd like to come, the sooner the better.'

'I can come any time, Mr Jameson.'

'Well then, not tomorrow, but how about the day after?'

'Perfect.'

'How about eleven in the morning?'

'That would be fine.'

'Right. Goodbye.'

The line went dead before Stella had a chance to say her own goodbye. The abrupt dismissal reminded her of her father – 'dislike wasting time on non-essentials' – and she wondered if all men in their fifties, if they were single, became increasingly self-contained.

He lived in a Georgian house set in about two acres of land. It had been built as a farmhouse in the early part of the nineteenth century by a farmer who had profited from the high price of corn. Outhouses and stables were attached to the main building. As she drove up a gravel

60

drive Stella wondered how he managed to run the house on his own. Later she learned that his sister was part of the household. She didn't meet the sister but at one stage caught sight of a thin woman dressed completely in black, grey hair scraped tightly into a bun which accentuated a long, pale face, before the woman ducked into a doorway out of sight.

'My sister is a bit of a recluse,' Jameson had explained. 'She's shy with people she doesn't know.'

He too was tall and thin with a long face which reminded Stella of a celebrated portrait of Philip IV of Spain by Velasquez. Dressed in tweeds, leather elbow patches on the jacket, and wearing a shirt with stiffly starched white collar which emphasised the scraggy flesh of his neck, he seemed more than one generation removed from the woman who had been his mistress. His welcome was courteous. He asked about traffic conditions on the journey and enquired whether she would like any refreshment, a cup of tea perhaps, before inspecting his garden.

She accepted the offer of tea and he disappeared for five minutes leaving her to look around the high-ceilinged drawing room. All fabric furnishings were faded but of best quality and the woodwork had the deep glow which comes from years of polishing. The housepride in Stella noted and approved. Oil paintings of still lifes hung on the walls but these had been neglected. Fruit and flowers which once must have been bright and fresh were dulled by a dark patina of ancient dust and smoke motes from an impressive marble fireplace.

Except for electric light fittings nothing in the room seemed to belong to the twentieth century. Outside it was a hot August day but the room remained cool. All right in summer, Stella thought, but without central heating the house was probably an ice-box in winter. It wasn't easy to reconcile a glossy photograph of a warm-blooded young woman with the peculiarly life-less atmosphere of the place.

Jameson returned with a tray of bone china and Georgian silver and asked if she would care to pour out tea. He went and sat in a wing chair which had antimacassars on back and sides and she was aware of his unwavering stare as she poured the tea. It gave her the uncomfortable feeling that he had shed the role of polite host and was deliberately trying to disconcert her. Her attempts at conversation – the weather, the peaceful setting of the house, how she enjoyed his book – were withered by spare, non-committal replies. And then, when she was searching desperately for something to say he fired the question, 'Why did you choose wild flowers for your children's project?'

'These days it's not easy to pick a subject which someone won't find controversial or objectionable, and while I was gardening I couldn't make up my mind whether to treat the golden rod which had sowed itself as a garden flower or treat it as a weed.'

'And what did you decide?'

'I left it. If it had the life force to flourish in a bed which hydrangeas regarded as their own it deserved to survive. And I thought – why not wild flowers as a subject.'

She spoke a sort of truth constructed from patches of smaller truths, but it was also a prepared statement for such a question. He gave a slight nod of approval and she felt she had passed some sort of test.

'Wild flowers are wilful,' he said. 'Clever too. Have you ever noticed how the really small flowers will group themselves together so as to make themselves notice-able by pollinating insects?'

He warmed to the subject of survival, speaking of wild flowers, and their need to be saved from the depredations of chemical pollution, with the passionate enthusiasm of an evangelist.

When he showed her round the garden she was surprised by its order. It was laid out in a number of oblong plots like a formal garden. In a far corner a young man was digging.

'You have some help, I see,' she said.

'I need it. Daryll is as strong as an ox. Been in a bit of trouble in his time but he's marvellously gentle with flowers and animals.'

As if sensing that he was being talked about the man looked across and raised his hand. Then he carried on digging slamming the spade's blade into the soil with renewed ferocity.

'Let me explain my system,' said Jameson. He went on to tell her that various species needed different types of soil and he accommodated this by providing supplements of chalk, sand, gravel or stone. Some parts of the garden were fairly dry; others marshy.

'What started as a hobby has become a business,' he said. 'I sell to a producer of macrobiotic foods and also to a company which specialises in homeopathic medicine. What I don't sell can flourish in its own way and I hope seeds will be carried by wind, bird or insect to other parts of the country to replace stock lost through the ravages of urban development and motorways.'

'I shouldn't think you're very popular with your neighbours,' remarked Stella with a light laugh, looking at a mass of dandelions.

'Don't give a damn about neighbours,' he answered unsmilingly. 'Do them good to cultivate a few dandelions themselves. *Taraxacum officinale*. Marvellous diuretic. Rich in potassium. You make the leaves into a tea.'

They were strolling back towards the house. After a long pause he said, 'But to do my neighbours credit they didn't come snooping around like some. They kept a distance. That was after the tragedy.' He shot a quick glance at her. 'But you know about that?'

'A tragedy?'

63

He didn't reply but led the way into the house and they returned to the drawing room. 'Are you in a hurry to go?' he asked.

'No, I've plenty of time. All day.'

'But you'll want to get back to your husband.'

'Well, yes. But I've still got time to spare.'

'What about the dog?'

'I've left the windows down and he has a bowl of water.'

Jameson sat down in the wing armchair and she took a chair opposite.

'Now then,' he said. 'What else would you like to know?'

She shifted in her seat. 'I've learned a lot,' she began.

'But you haven't learned what you came to learn, have you?'

'I'm not sure what you mean.'

'I think you are. When I decided to see you I thought you were a keen school teacher, nothing more. But then the name "Best" rang a bell. I did some checking. You and your husband were the ones who found my darling's body, were you not?'

She could feel her cheeks flushing and lowered her head. 'Yes,' she said quietly.

'And so – why are you here? What do you want to learn?'

She looked up. The cliché phrase 'My cover is blown' passed through her mind. Now or never. Come clean. Nothing to lose. 'There *is* a project,' she said slowly, 'and I have set it to the children. But I wanted to meet you too. And it seemed an opportunity . . .' Her voice tailed away.

'Why did you want to meet me? You don't strike me as one of those vultures who feed on the misfortunes of others.'

'It's not like that. I've . . . I've become involved . . . That is, I can't get Deirdre out of my mind.'

'Nor can I,' he murmured to himself. 'Why do you think you can't get her out of your mind?' he asked.

'I've no idea.' It was a feeble answer but she couldn't tell him it had started with Rodney's obsession and now she seemed to have been infected by it.

He gave her a long, penetrating look. 'You're not unlike,' he said at length. 'You and Deirdre could pass as sisters.'

'I feel flattered. She was quite a beauty.'

His eyes clouded and as if he were reciting an epitaph composed in sadness he said, 'She was the most beautiful flower in my garden. Heaven in a wild flower, as the poet says.' Apologetically he added, 'You must forgive me for being sentimental.' For a few seconds he was lost in thought. When he spoke again his voice was firm and his eyes clear. 'It isn't only looks. She had a physical approach to life which I think you may share.'

Stella guessed a compliment was intended but she wasn't sure she wanted to be likened to Deirdre in a physical approach to life. She plucked at her skirt, adjusting a fold.

'Speaking of wild flowers,' he went on, 'would you like a glass of elderberry wine? I don't have the usual alcoholic beverages to offer.'

'I've never tasted elderberry wine.'

'It's quite potent.'

'I'd like to try it.'

'Try anything once, as Deirdre used to say. Good. I'll join you.'

He left the room and returned with two glasses of dark red wine. She took a sip.

'Well,' he asked.

'Very nice,' she lied.

He nodded. 'Now then,' he said. 'What is it you want to know?'

'That's difficult. I just want to know more about Deirdre.'

'I could say it was none of your business, but I won't. Any more than it's your business how she and I got along in spite of her wild ways. But I'll tell you. I think we may find for different reasons we can each help the other in a search for the truth.' He paused. 'I loved Deirdre very much and her happiness was my desire. She needed freedom, not to be a bird in a gilded cage. I was happy to give her freedom so long as she was discreet. The arrangement worked well. She didn't let me down. She had the freedom she needed but she always came back to me, and I never asked questions. This was something the police found hard to understand. Not that she should come home, but that I wasn't angry or jealous. It was as well I had a cast-iron alibi.'

'Could I ask what it was?'

'You could. A company rep was here all afternoon. He didn't leave till after five and Deirdre was killed, so the police think, at three-fifteen . . . Next question please.' A faintly humorous look in his eyes travelled down his long face and ended as the wisp of a smile on his lips.

'I don't want to seem . . . probing.'

His smile widened. 'I'll tell you something. When I saw the police were getting nowhere I hired a private detective. I got a man who charges well over the fee recommended by the Institute of Private Investigators, but he has a reputation for success. When I got your letter I suspected there might be more in it than met the eye. It seemed odd a teacher should take so much trouble to get information for a holiday project. And why my book? There are more easily available books on the subject. And then your name rang a bell. I asked my chap to find out more about you. He confirmed that you and your husband were the Mr and Mrs Best who discovered Deirdre. And he went further. He found out that your husband had been with Deirdre when she made a commercial for television. Now tell me this. Does your husband know you've come to see me?'

'No.'

'I thought not. I won't say what I do think, but I can make a guess why, like me, you want to get at the truth. That's why I said we may be able to help each other because I can tell you that if it's the last thing I do I'll get whoever killed my darling. And when I do I'll crucify him.'

He spoke softly but his body was taut as a drawn bow-string and his words were shot like arrows.

'Have you any idea who might have killed her?' Stella asked.

The tension went out of him. He picked up his glass of wine and took a sip.

'An idea, yes. Proof, no.'

With a mouth suddenly dry she asked, 'Is there someone you suspect?'

'Yes.'

Almost inaudibly she asked, 'Who?'

He shook his head. 'That's one question I won't answer. I said we might be able to help each other. I didn't say we should disclose every single thought to each other. But I'll say this. Whoever has the bracelet Deirdre was wearing will have some very difficult questions to answer.'

'You think the murderer stole it?'

'I do. And I'll tell you why. That bracelet was heavy with gold charms. Now he wouldn't necessarily steal it for its value. If he was a common thief he'd have taken the watch too. No, he took the bracelet because some of the charms were custom made. Unique. Made by a goldsmith for a special customer. Find the bracelet and we find the goldsmith, and then we find the customer.'

She couldn't meet his intent gaze and the memory of a bracelet slipping out of a metal container was so vivid it paralysed all thought. After a long hesitation she said,

'I see. Yes.' Speech became easier. 'But I don't know how I can help in that direction.'

'Think about it. You may find you can.'

She finished the wine and stood up. 'It's been most kind of you to have helped with the project.'

'No need to hurry off. Would you like something to eat?'

'No, thanks. I must go.'

As she moved towards the door he got to his feet with an agility that belied his age. 'You will tell me if you have any ideas, won't you? We must co-operate on this.'

'Yes, I will.'

'As I said earlier, we both have the same objective even if our motives are different. We want Deirdre's murderer found and brought to justice.'

She wanted to run. The stale atmosphere of the room was oppressive and she felt she could hardly breathe. But using all her willpower she went with him slowly towards the front door, making polite, trivial talk about his garden when what she most wanted was never to see the garden again.

They shook hands.

'Thank you for seeing me,' she said.

'On the contrary. Thank you for coming . . . I think the quarry will soon be in my sights.'

SEVEN

Doubts which had been suppressed flooded into her mind once more. William Jameson had treated her as some sort of ally in a search for truth but it wasn't a dispassionate search, he was more like a hunter stalking prey. He obviously suspected someone. Who? The man who had found Deirdre's body?

Does the criminal always return to the scene of his crime?

Her father might know the answer. Or would he say, 'Silly cliché. Not supported by statistics.'

The bracelet. It was symbol, clue and key. Symbol of Deirdre's life-style; clue to who might have killed her; and key to Rodney's strange behaviour.

The day after their bitter argument she had checked the steel container. The bracelet had been removed. Where had he hidden it? Or had he disposed of it, thrown it, wrapped in untraceable paper, on to a rubbish tip?

She would search the house and if she didn't find the damned bracelet she would have to decide whether to stake her marriage on another confrontation.

In guilty haste, hearing attuned to catch the sound of his early return, she went through all the drawers in his study and then went systematically through every room in the house looking for places where the bracelet might be concealed. Finally, she went into the loft and examined rafters and cross beams for any secret cache. Her search drew a blank. If he still possessed the bracelet it wasn't in the house.

The phone rang. He wouldn't be home until late. A couple of Danes, potential customers, had arrived one day earlier than expected and he had to take them out. Entertaining foreign customers was a new chore and one which still held the shine of novelty. It entailed expense account dinners at good restaurants and, if the customer desired, drinks at a night club where lights were low and waitresses topless. Once or twice customers had asked if it was possible to arrange a girl for the night and Rodney had taken them to bars notorious for having among the clientele young and beautiful women who for a substantial fee provided services to satisfy a variety of whims and fantasies.

Recently he had been given the brief of 'customer relations' in addition to the job of regional sales manager. It brought him a step closer to becoming a director and although it could produce hassle, as when an aircraft arrived late from the continent, he was sufficiently ambitious to put up with such inconveniences. He might grumble to Stella but she knew he never complained at the company's offices.

She was awake when he came home in the early hours but she feigned sleep. She heard him whisper, 'Are you awake?'

She breathed slowly and regularly.

'Stella, are you awake?'

A pause. She heard him sigh and then, without switching on the light, he began to undress and he didn't attempt to keep quiet. My God, she thought, if I had been asleep I'd have been awake by now.

He tried one last time. 'Are you awake, darling?' Then he got into bed and thankfully didn't try his sometimes trick of inching closer and closer until some part of her body felt the pressure of male virility.

At breakfast the following morning she asked how the evening had been.

70

'A bit of a bore. I wasn't really in the mood but these Danes certainly were. I thought Denmark was a permissive paradise and they wouldn't want what they did want. I was amazed. Don't they get enough in Copenhagen, I asked myself. Perhaps the fact of being away from wives and families is the answer. I don't know whether absence makes the heart grow fonder but it didn't half perk up their libidos.'

'Did you manage to fix them up?'

'Oh, yes. A couple of birds with a taste for champagne.'

She gave him a quick glance over the rim of a coffee cup. 'And you? Didn't you want to join the fun?'

'Fun! Not my idea of fun.' He wiped his hands on a napkin. 'But I shan't be late tonight, I hope. I thought we might go out.'

'Yes, if you like.'

He gave an odd smile, reached down, and passed a small parcel across the table. It was gift-wrapped. 'Happy anniversary,' he said.

Colour rose to her cheeks. 'Happy anniversary,' she replied. 'I'm afraid I haven't got you anything.' She hoped he wouldn't guess she had forgotten it was their wedding anniversary. It was received folklore that husbands were neglectful of special dates which wives had engraved on their hearts.

'That's all right,' she heard him say.

'Can I open it?'

'Why not? It's nothing explosive.'

Her fingers fumbled at the gold ribbon and it might have been the colour, or an echo of her worry, but the ribbon reminded her of the bracelet and for a horrifying moment she thought the parcel might contain a bracelet. It might even be Deirdre's bracelet.

Inside the wrapping was a small brown box. She opened the box, half-fearful of what she might see. It was a relief to see a brooch set with a stone having black and white parallel bands.

71

'An onyx,' she said.

'Right. In the language of gems it's supposed to insure married happiness. And it's your birth stone.'

'For July? I didn't realise . . . It's lovely.' She came round the table to kiss him.

He pulled her close and would have tried to turn the kiss into something more but she drew away. 'I do wish I'd got something for you.'

'There's only . . .' he began and broke off.

'What?'

'Nothing.'

She knew what he had almost said was, 'There's only one thing I want from you and you're giving it less and less these days.'

'You weren't awake when I came in,' he said.

'No. I didn't hear a thing. You must have been very quiet.'

'I tried to be quiet.' He poured himself a second cup of coffee. 'If you'd been awake I was going to tell you about something that's been bugging me for the last few days.'

All her faculties became alert. 'What's that?'

'I think I'm being followed.' He shook his head. 'It doesn't make sense, I know. Why should anyone follow me? But I think I'm being tailed. And by some sort of heavy.'

Immediately she thought of the detective hired by William Jameson.

'How can you be sure?' she asked. 'He can't be much of a tail if you know he's there.'

'That's just it. I don't think he cares if I know he's watching me. It's almost deliberate intimidation.'

'You could ask what he wants.'

'I did. Yesterday. He was hanging around the car park when I left with the Danes. I went across and asked what the idea was. Following me around. He gave a mean look and said, "It's a free country. I can go where I want."'

'What did you say to that?' she asked, giving him a

72

curious look.

'What could I say. He'd have laughed if I'd told him to get lost. Anyway, I couldn't keep my customers waiting.'

'Was he a big man?'

'Very.'

'A good thing you had the Danes with you.'

He frowned. 'The same thing crossed my mind. I'm not afraid. Don't think that. But you can never tell.'

She gave the ghost of a smile, the sort of smile which reflects inner amusement. Then, serious once more, she asked, 'Could it be something to do with your job?'

'I sell soups, not government secrets.'

'Then what?'

'Search me.' He raised his arms as if inviting her to go through his pockets.

'It couldn't be . . . No, it couldn't be . . .' She broke off hoping he would pick up the thread of doubt in her voice.

He obliged. 'What? Couldn't be what?'

'The bracelet.'

'The bracelet?'

'Deirdre's.'

His face became impassive. She sensed doors being locked and bolted. 'I don't follow you.'

'Well, it's obviously valuable and whoever gave it to her might suspect that you, the one who found her, might have taken it and wants it back.'

'I shouldn't think so.'

'Why not? It might be incriminating evidence in some way. Suppose the murderer gave it her and he wants it back because he's afraid it might be traced to him.'

'If that's so, I don't see the point of letting me know I'm being followed.'

She shrugged.

'It's just a bracelet with charms,' he said.

'They might be traceable.'

He glanced at his watch and stood up. 'I'd better be going.'

'Where is it?' she asked.

'What?'

She rolled her eyes upwards. 'The bracelet, of course. What else?'

He gave a look of studied coolness. 'I haven't got it. I don't know where it is now. And I must go. See you this evening.'

He darted round the table and gave her a light kiss that scarcely fanned her cheek.

'Thanks for the pressie,' she said. 'It's lovely.'

He paused on his way to the door. 'Perhaps I should have made it a bracelet. You seem to covet it.'

She winced and he was gone.

Norman Selkey was a thin, nervous man who wore gold-rimmed spectacles. Through a magnifying eye-glass he examined the Lincoln Imp while Stella stood on the other side of the counter in his jeweller's shop.

'It's gold,' Selkey said. 'Twenty-two carat and has the standard mark used on British made wares since 1975. I can't make out the sponsor's mark. It could be a "p".' He scrutinised the charm even more closely. 'I can make out the leopard's head and so we have the London assay office.' He removed the eye-glass. 'More than that, Mrs Best, I cannot say.'

'You don't stock these?'

'Oh, yes, but not this particular charm. Most unusual. I've never seen one like it.'

'Who might have made it?'

Selkey gave a nervous smile. 'I can't even venture a guess.'

'Is there any way I could find out?'

Selkey's smile was fixed and he spoke through it. 'You might try Goldsmiths' Hall. That's where the mark should be registered, but it won't necessarily lead you to the maker. The mark may represent a wholesaler or a retailer.'

74

She picked up the charm from the counter. 'Thank you very much, Mr Selkey.'

'A pleasure, Mrs Best.'

She put the charm in her handbag and left the shop. The moment the door closed after her the smile was wiped from Selkey's face. He hurried to a back room and began foraging among papers on a table.

Once or twice he heard a doorbell ring as a customer entered the shop and heard the voice of his assistant saying 'Good morning' and he paused in his search to listen for the customer's request.

When he found the paper he was looking for, a list widely circulated to jewellers, he took a deep breath and began reading. As he had thought, among the listed items of a stolen charm bracelet a Lincoln Imp was mentioned. He was sweating slightly. He took off his spectacles, wiped them, and read again. The words 'Lincoln Imp' were between 'Witch on a broomstick' and 'Boot with a high heel'.

The door opened and a young woman with blonde hair dark at the roots appeared. 'Mr Selkey, do we have any silver buckles? A lady says her daughter has just become an SRN and wants a silver buckle for her belt.'

'Third drawer down, below the till.'

'Thanks.' The woman disappeared.

Dilemma. Report to the police that someone had come with a Lincoln Imp which might belong to the missing bracelet and thereby risk losing a good customer, or do nothing. He thought for a moment and visualised his dead mother. In his head he heard her voice speaking clearly, 'You must follow your conscience, Cyril.'

His lips framed the words, 'Yes, Mother,' and with a trembling hand reached for the telephone.

'Go on, Cyril,' said a ghostly voice in his head.

When the call was connected he said breathlessly, 'I'd like to speak to Detective Inspector Cook, please.'

EIGHT

After her visit to Selkey she went to the local library to find out about goldsmiths from reference books. There could only be a limited number working in and around London and it shouldn't be too difficult by a process of elimination to track down the maker of the charm.

She learned that the Worshipful Company of Goldsmiths was one of the great livery companies of the City of London and its guild had been formed in the thirteenth century. It had been instrumental in the introduction of paper currency and was also the benefactor of educational foundations. The schoolmistress seam in her was exposed to the pleasure of gaining knowledge on a subject previously unquarried – it occurred to her that here was a topic for a future holiday project – and, without realising it, time passed quickly in reading of the art and work of goldsmiths. It was only when she came across a reference to the manufacture of gold jewellery being carried on in the Clerkenwell district of London that she returned to the task in hand. Were there still goldsmiths in Clerkenwell?

She obtained a copy of the London Yellow Pages telephone directory but the area it covered was limited to north London. A copy for central London, in which Clerkenwell would be listed, was not available. Nevertheless she found three working goldsmiths in the north London area. She might do worse than begin her enquiries with these.

On her way home she stopped in the town centre for some shopping and it was early in the afternoon before she drove down the road where she and Rodney lived. As she approached their house she was surprised to see a car parked near the driveway. She had to swerve in a wide arc to avoid it and, in passing, she threw an angry glance at the driver who was quite unconcerned by the inconvenience he'd caused. He nodded at her and smiled. It was Detective Inspector Cook.

He was standing in the driveway when she came out of the garage.

'Good afternoon, Mrs Best.'

Her heart began to beat uncomfortably fast, but coolly, and with an edge of sarcasm, she said, 'I hope I haven't kept you waiting.'

'In my job one gets used to it. You know the saying, "It all comes to he who waits."'

'You wanted to see me?'

He gave a smile which would have withered the confidence of any criminal. 'If you could spare a few minutes,' he said.

She was holding a bag containing her shopping. 'I want to dump this. You'd better come in.'

He followed her.

Indoors, they stood in the hall. She was in no mood to be sociable and after putting down her bag she asked bluntly, 'What is it you want?'

'It's very simple. I won't take a moment.'

She gave an impatient shrug. 'I am fairly busy.'

'Busy making enquiries?'

'Why do you say that?'

'Mrs Best, I have only one question to ask. It is this. Where did you get a small Lincoln Imp charm?'

Her heart was now beating so fast it seemed to have grown wings which were lifting it into her throat, and her voice had a breathless note. 'I'm sorry. I don't understand.'

He was not smiling now. 'Please don't prevaricate. I know you have such a charm. Where did you get it?'

'I found it.'

'Where?' The question was fired like a bullet.

'I found it . . . I found it on the roadside.'

'Where on the roadside?'

Her mind seemed to be operating in overdrive.

'The day my husband and I found Deirdre Jameson's body. While we were waiting for the police to arrive I noticed it in the gutter.'

'And you didn't report your find?'

'Why should I?'

He shook his head slowly as though she were a new but very dull police recruit. 'You could be accused of stealing by finding. You must have known it had value. You should have reported your find.'

'Perhaps I should.'

'Particularly since you must have known that it might have belonged to the deceased.'

She avoided his eyes. 'I'm afraid that didn't occur to me. I put it in my pocket and forgot about it. It was only yesterday I discovered it . . . I suppose you heard about it from Mr Selkey?'

'Like the Press we don't disclose sources of information without permission.'

'It doesn't matter.' She looked straight at him. 'Is that all?'

'You realise the charm you allege you found by the roadside belonged to Deirdre Jameson?'

'Certainly. If you say so.'

'I must ask you for it. I'll give you a receipt.'

With an expression of blank indifference on her face she opened her handbag and took out a twist of tissue paper. He was already writing a receipt on a page from his notebook.

'Funny little fellow. An imp if I ever saw one,' he remarked after unwrapping the tissue. 'A good thing Mr

78

Jameson was able to give us a full inventory of what was on the bracelet. Was this the only one you found "by the roadside"? Or were there others?'

'The only one,' she said firmly.

They were facing each other in the small front hall. He peered past her as if looking for something. 'And you've no idea where the other charms or the bracelet might be? Please think before you answer.'

She resented being treated as though she were slightly stupid and with the self-induced indignation of the guilty under pressure she snapped, 'I don't need time for thought. I haven't the slightest idea where the other charms might be.'

'Very strange that just one should have found its way to the roadside and all the others be missing. Do you think it hopped there on its one leg?'

'I don't think that's very funny.'

'I'm not trying to be funny. I'm trying to ascertain facts.'

You're trying to provoke me, she thought. 'It could have broken off,' she said.

'Broken off?'

'Come loose from the bracelet.'

He weighed her reply. 'Very odd that only one should "come loose".'

'I've nothing else to suggest. And now, if that's all, I am busy.'

'Did your husband know you'd found a charm by the roadside, or did you pick it up and put it in your pocket while he wasn't looking?'

She was thrown by the question. Rodney mustn't be drawn into this line of enquiry. Her hesitation before replying was swiftly exploited.

'It seems you do need time for thought, Mrs Best. Strange. I would have thought you could have answered that one immediately.'

'I can't remember. No. I think he was a little way off.

He wouldn't have noticed. And then the police car arrived and the whole thing slipped my mind.'

Cook gave a supercilious smile before slowly repeating her words. 'He wouldn't have noticed. He was a little way off and wouldn't have noticed . . . I assume he knows about it now. Perhaps it was his idea that you should take it to a jeweller. Was it, Mrs Best?'

She felt her knees beginning to shake and wanted to sit down but to have done so might make him think he'd driven her into a corner. She must keep standing.

'I took it to Mr Selkey off my own bat,' she said. 'My husband doesn't know about it.'

'But you'll tell him?'

'I expect so.'

'You expect so.' Cook gave a grim smile as if she'd cracked an off-colour joke. 'Your husband will no doubt wonder, as I must confess I wonder, why you should want to know who the maker of the charm might be. I understand you weren't trying to sell it, you simply wanted to trace its maker. Is that right?'

He seemed enormous. A huge looming presence which filled the hall and would crush her into the wall. A giant of a man who could demolish anything that stood in his way.

Her voice whispered, 'Yes.'

'Why did you want to trace its maker, Mrs Best?'

She tried to step back, to put space between them, only to find her back was already pressing against the wall.

'Why, Mrs Best? Why?'

'Because . . . Because . . .' She searched frantically for a convincing lie.

'You must have known it was valuable,' said Cook, but in trying to increase the pressure he gave her an outlet.

'Yes, that's right. I knew it was valuable. I knew it must belong to someone. Someone who treasured it. It could have sentimental value. I thought if I could trace who made it I might be able to find its owner and return it.'

'How very thoughtful of you!'

The titan began to shrink and resume normal size. She sensed she was beginning to win the battle of wits. But her adversary had one more thrust. 'I'll leave you to your business now, but I should like to speak to your husband. He'll be in some time this evening, I assume?'

'Yes.'

'Good. I may look in if that's not too inconvenient.'

'It might be. I mean, it would be. We're going out tonight.'

'I see. Then some other time. Good day, Mrs Best.'

The afternoon dragged. She had no stomach for contacting goldsmiths and no stomach for food. The last thing she wanted was an anniversary treat but at least this had avoided a call from Detective Inspector Cook. But he would return, again and again, until he had winkled out the truth. Like someone besieged, she would have to defend a fortress built on the sand of lies.

What should she say to Rodney? Tell him that the imp had fallen on the floor when she found the bracelet?

By nature she liked to 'have things out in the open' but she was deterred by the fear that 'the open' would not be some sunlit pasture but a black forest of suspicion in which a nightmare lay in ambush.

The afternoon ended with her still undecided what action to take, and when she heard Rodney's key turn in the door she felt something akin to panic.

'I'm home,' he called.

As usual he went straight to the drinks cabinet for his unwinding drink. 'I've booked a table,' he said. 'I hope you're hungry. I am.'

'Good day?' she asked.

'Not bad. One thing bugged me though.'

'What was that?'

'You remember what I told you this morning. About

81

someone following me.'

Her heart sunk. 'Yes.'

'I saw him again today, but this time he sheered off when he spotted he'd been noticed.'

This is it, she thought. I must tell him.

'Could it be something to do with Deirdre?' she asked.

'Why should it?'

'The bracelet.'

His face hardened. 'You've got an obsession with that bracelet. It was the last thing I heard about this morning and just about the first thing when I get home.'

She steeled herself. Now or never. Out in the open. No more lies. 'There is a reason,' she said. 'When I found it one of the charms fell on the bathroom floor. I couldn't fasten it back.'

He tipped back his drink and began pouring another.

'It was a little gold imp,' she said.

'So you've got the Lincoln Imp.'

'You knew it was missing?'

He turned towards her. 'I knew. But go on. There's more, isn't there?'

'Yes. I can't get this business out of my mind. It's beginning to get me down. I'm thinking of it almost all the time.'

'Thinking of what?'

'Deirdre's death . . . Who killed her.'

'And you believe it's me.'

'No, I don't.' Her reply was a cry of despair. 'You didn't. You said you didn't.'

'Right. I didn't kill Deirdre Jameson.'

'But how did you get the bracelet?'

'I took it from her dead body.'

'But how . . . I mean, did you know where she was? That she'd been murdered?'

He didn't answer at once but said, 'Sorry, I never asked you. Would you like a drink?'

'No, thanks.'

82

'Why not? We might as well stay in and drink. It would be a mockery to go out on an anniversary celebration.'

'How did you know she'd been murdered?' Stella persisted. 'And when did you take the bracelet? When you and Max found the body, or earlier?'

'I can't answer that.'

'You mean you won't.'

'That's right. I won't.'

'You're protecting someone, aren't you?'

'Are you sure you don't want a drink?'

'I don't want to spend the evening drinking,' she said. 'I'm sorry if you think I've spoiled the day but it hasn't exactly been a wonderful day for me.'

'Oh? Why not?'

'I took the imp to Mr Selkey, the jeweller at the corner of the High Street. I wanted to find out about it. If its maker could be traced then perhaps the person who gave it to Deirdre could be traced and that might lead to whoever gave her the bracelet and' – she lowered her voice – 'to whoever killed her.'

He went to a chair and slumped into it. 'Playing detective?' he asked caustically.

'Yes, if you like. The trouble is . . .'

He sat up. 'Trouble?'

'Selkey informed the police. I had a visit from Inspector Cook this afternoon. I told him I'd found the imp by the roadside but he didn't believe me. At least, I don't think he believed me. He said he wanted to see you again.'

'Why should he want to see me? What have you said?'

'Nothing. Only what I've told you. I think he wants to check whether you knew I'd picked up the imp or whether my playing detective, as you call it, is something I'm doing on my own.'

'Great,' he said wearily. 'There's nothing I like better than to have personal attention from our wonderful police. I guess he relieved you of the imp.'

'He gave me a receipt for it.'

'I'm sure he did. He's doing it by the book. And the police will find out who made it.'

'But does that matter?'

'It matters quite a bit,' he said. 'You might as well know. I can't stop the wheels turning. You're bound to know eventually. The man who gave Deirdre the Lincoln Imp and some of the other charms was your father.'

A CHARMED DEATH
Part 2

ONE

Ambrose Mytton, senior partner in a firm of London solicitors, had been born in Lincoln. His father owned a drapery store and was a man of few words. During his life he intimidated his wife and children and Ambrose grew up in a household of strict Sunday observance and long silences. Any merriment was quenched by the reproof, 'laughter of the fool', drawn from a verse in Ecclesiastes. All speech was monitored for superfluity. To use one word too many was to invite the comment that one was wasting one's breath. Ambrose became an inhibited child.

He was fifteen before he first defied his father. He pointed out that breath could not be wasted. Breathing was involuntary. If waste existed it was a waste of thought on the part of the speaker and of time for the listener. His father considered this proposition and instead of a stern rebuff Ambrose was surprised to hear him say, 'That is logical. You shall be a lawyer.'

In adult life Ambrose might have rebelled against his upbringing and become garrulous, but he found it useful in his profession to acquire a reputation for laconic utterance and a severe sense of moral honesty. If his image verged on the eccentric, there was no harm in this. Eccentrics are rewarded by notice, and lawyers who specialise in litigation usually profit from being noticed as many famous advocates, past and present, have discovered.

Ambrose admired the condensed speech patterns of King George V and Clement Attlee, and he liked General Franco's custom of standing to attention when receiving a visitor so that the impress of extreme formality was put on a meeting which the visitor had thought would be a friendly get-together. There had been many young articled clerks from other firms who, meeting him for the first time, had been disconcerted by seeing a senior solicitor spring to his feet and be greeted by the words, 'Good morning, sir,' with heavy emphasis on the 'sir'. Ambrose distanced people. He distanced even his wife who conceived Stella after a coition so brief she didn't have time to look at the ceiling and think of England.

Regularly once a month both before and after his wife's death Ambrose visited an address in Mayfair where, at the hands of an erotically clad lady, he received what was euphemistically called 'relief', but his emotions weren't involved. It was an appointment on a par with paying a visit to a doctor's surgery for a necessary prescription. There were only two people with whom he had ever been truly close and allowed warmth and emotional spontaneity to colour the relationship; one was his daughter, the other was Deirdre Jameson.

On the day the television commercial was due to be made Ambrose Mytton had to attend a court in Birmingham. He and Rodney travelled together in Ambrose's car. The court case finished earlier than expected and he went to the studio to collect Rodney. The commercial was still in process of being made. 'Takes a whole day to make five seconds of film,' said Ambrose disapprovingly. 'Wasteful of time and money.' But it was the only adverse comment he made.

Mistaking long silences of the older man for the silence of boredom Rodney apologised that the filming was taking so long.

'Don't worry. Finding it interesting.'

He was speaking to Rodney but looking elsewhere. Rodney followed the fixed gaze. It rested on the young woman who was smilingly holding up a can of soup to the camera.

He had never got along well with his father-in-law but decided to take a chance. 'Would you like to meet her?' he asked.

'What?'

'Be introduced to the star of our commercial?'

The older man said, 'Wouldn't object,' without hesitation.

When the filming was finished Rodney invited Deirdre Jameson to join him and Ambrose for a meal at a nearby hotel.

To any observer it must have seemed a strange little dinner party. The two younger people seemed to inhabit a separate world from the older man who spoke and ate sparingly. He might have been a stranger who, due to overbooking, had been accommodated at their table.

Towards the end of the meal Rodney was summoned to take a phone call. He returned looking serious. A message from head office, routed via the film agency, requested him to go north as soon as possible. An emergency had arisen in Leeds where a director of Susan's Starters had dropped dead in the middle of clinching a deal. It was essential that his papers relating to profit margins were retrieved as soon as possible.

'I can hire a car,' he said to Ambrose, 'but I'll have to leave at once. Will you look after Deirdre? We'll square up later.'

'Pleasure. Be on your way. See you back in town.'

'Sorry about this,' Rodney said to Deirdre.

'Not to worry,' she smiled. 'Business comes first.'

'Bye then.' He raised his hand and left the table, almost bumping into a waiter in his haste.

A short silence was broken by Ambrose. 'Stuck with me then.'

She gave a brilliant smile. 'Stuck nothing. I prefer the company of older men.'

'Did you mean what you said? Business comes first?'

'Of course. I always mean what I say. I can't bear people who say one thing and mean another. Can you?'

'No."

She laughed. 'That's positive.' She tilted her head slightly; it was a movement engagingly expressive of curiosity. 'Are you always so positive? A straight yes or no? I've noticed you haven't spoken much.'

'No point in speaking unless there's something worthwhile saying.'

'Oh, come on. I don't agree with that. I'll bet all the things that are ever worth saying could all be said in half an hour. So what do you do with the rest of your life? Join a contemplative Order?'

'Why not?' The question was sharp but his eyes were twinkling.

'I'll tell you why not. Because life is meant to be lived, and lived to the full. We only live once – and that's something worth saying, and repeating.'

'Hm.' He looked at her hand. 'Married?'

She lifted her hand and stretched the fingers. His gaze was riveted on their slender shape tapering into blood-red nails. 'No ring on the third finger. See.'

'I see.'

She lifted her other hand. A gold bracelet with five charms circled her wrist. 'This is my ring of gold.' She shook her wrist so that the charms jiggled. 'Life,' she said.

'Don't follow your drift.'

She laughed again. He found it an entrancing sound. She lifted her left hand, bare except for a ring on the little finger. 'This is one side of me.' She lifted the other hand and shook the bracelet. 'This is the other.'

The twinkle in his eyes had become a gleam. 'Two sides to you?'

'Don't you have two sides?'

'Can't say I have. Makes me seem a dull chap.'
She shook her head. 'Not dull, but maybe a late starter.'
'Late starter, eh? You may be right.'
She gave a little smile and turned her head away. His
eyes feasted on her profile. Ambrose Mytton was falling
in love.
She turned back suddenly and caught his gaze. Her
eyes widened slightly. She knew what was happening.
'You're a lawyer then,' she said.
'That's right.'
'I must be careful. Lawyers can trip you up.'
'I hope you don't think . . .'
'I was teasing,' she interrupted. 'But it's best to tell the
truth, the whole truth and nothing but the truth when
you're with a lawyer, isn't it?'
'Lawyers prefer it.'
'I won't tell you all my boring life story,' she said.
'Only the last bit. I'm divorced. My ex-husband has
custody of our two kids. The man I live with is a good
man, much older than me. He's the sort that likes
helping lame dogs over stiles. Not that I'm lame. But he
humours me. I think he'd like me to give up the acting
stuff and maybe I will if there's going to be a fuss about
union membership. As for this,' she held up her hand
with the bracelet circling the wrist. 'This is the past. I
won't let you into my lurid secrets, but it reminds me that
at least I've had a past. I wouldn't want to go to the grave
not knowing what it's all about.'
'I'm glad you told me,' said Ambrose.
'Told you about what?'
'Your marriage. Children. That you have – a past.'
'Why? Does it interest you? My past?'
He knew she was gently mocking him. He knew some
sort of bait was being offered. And he wanted bait. He
was a fish which had swum too long in isolation. He
wanted to be hooked. He was a fish searching for a hook.
'Your future interests me, too,' he said.

91

'Why? You hardly know me.'

'That's my misfortune,' he murmured.

'Flatterer.' She turned towards him and fluttered her eyelashes, parodying a silent screen coquette. But he was no Valentino to respond with lambent-eyed yearning. He cleared his throat, fiddled with his table napkin, and eventually managed to say, 'Compliment. Not flattery.'

'Well, thank you. And you? Married of course. How many children?'

'Widower. Just one child. Stella. Rodney's wife.'

'She close to you? Your daughter?'

'Oh, yes.'

'It was the same with me. I used to sit on my Dad's knee and he'd tell me stories.'

And so they continued to talk, she skilfully leading him from one topic to another, giving the right feedback, agreeing when she sensed it was important to agree, and disagreeing when she knew it would evoke his admiration for her independence of thought. They had coffee and a liqueur, and then more coffee, and were almost the last to leave.

'How are you getting home?' he asked.

'I've got my car down the road.'

His face fell. 'I could have given you a lift. Not far out of my way. Never mind.' They were now in the hotel foyer. 'It's been most enjoyable meeting you. Perhaps we'll meet again some day.'

'I'd like that,' she said. 'I really would.'

'You mean that?'

'Of course I mean it. You, being a lawyer, are supposed to remember everything that's said. Don't you remember me saying I always meant what I said?'

'Yes. You're right.' He felt for his wallet and produced a card. 'If ever you're in London . . .' He handed her the card.

'Got a pen?' she asked.

'Yes.'

'And a bit of paper. I'll give you my number and if ever you're up my way . . .' She looked at him and gave him the works, the full come-hither treatment, with her eyes. 'Thursday is always a good day for me.'

He drove back to London with her parting look scorched on his memory.

Within a fortnight he had found an excuse to travel north. It happened to be on a Thursday. She answered the phone.

'Ambrose Mytton,' he announced.

'Ambrose!' She sounded delighted. 'I was thinking of you a few minutes ago.'

'Wondered if you'd be free for a drink. Perhaps something to eat.'

'I'd love that. Where are you?'

He named a village a few miles from Ipswich.

'I know it,' she said. 'There's a pub called the Cock. I'll meet you there in about half an hour.'

It was the first of a series of meetings, usually five or six weeks apart but always on a Thursday, the day when William Jameson went, in all weathers, in search of fresh plants. They would meet in the car park of the Cock Inn and she would get into his car and they would drive off to some other, more remote pub, until one day in summer she arrived with a picnic basket containing half a cold chicken, bread rolls and salad, a bottle of hock and a flask of coffee.

'I thought it would be nice on such a lovely day to find some quiet spot,' she said. 'The hock's been on ice all morning and there's more ice in the basket.'

They studied the map and set off for a place called Santer's Wood. Down a lane, and past the wood, they came to a stream. Leaving the car by a bridge they took the picnic basket along the bank of the stream until they found a secluded spot near a clump of silver birches. He had brought a travelling rug which he spread on the ground.

The setting was idyllic and Ambrose for the first time in many years experienced a feeling of total contentment. All the pressures of his everyday existence were forgotten; everything except the present moment seemed trivial and meaningless. He was hopelessly, foolishly, abjectly in love with Deirdre Jameson. It was calf love in September. If she had demanded that he jumped fully clothed into the stream and sing the national anthem backwards he would have done his best to oblige.

'The hock is delicious,' he said, 'but if I'd known what you were planning I'd have brought champagne.'

'Champagne next time,' she said.

He was so ridiculously in love that the implication that there would be a next time thrilled him to the core.

'Here,' she said. 'I've got the wishbone. Pull it with me.'

She was holding the fragile bone in the crook of her little finger. He took the free stem and pulled.

'You've got it,' she said, handing him the smaller piece. 'Put them together, close your eyes and wish.'

He did as he was told. As their relationship had ripened she had subtly assumed control. She did the telling, and he did as he was told. For a man who played the role of boss in the office and had always been master of the house at home it was delightful to be gently dominated by a woman half his age.

He closed his eyes.

'Have you wished?' she asked.

'Yes.'

'I won't ask what it was. It wouldn't come true. You want it to come true, do you?'

'Very much.'

'That sounds intriguing. I won't spoil it by asking what it was but it's fair to ask if it concerns someone or something.'

94

'Someone.'

'I'm not going to ask who. I probably wouldn't know her anyway.'

'But you do.'

She smothered a laugh. 'You are lovely.'

'Lovely?' He was bewildered.

She closed the basket, put it to one side, finished her glass of wine, and lay down on her back. 'Kiss me,' she said, 'and that's an order.'

At a point near the point of no return he gasped, 'Is it safe?'

'Don't worry.'

He closed his eyes, abandoned all restraint, and thrust his way towards the brief sweet oblivion of climax. When he opened his eyes she was smiling up at him. And then, quite suddenly, her expression changed and he felt her body jerk rhythmically below him.

Later, when they were clearing away the debris of their meal he said, 'I want to give you something.'

'You already have!'

'I mean a present.'

'A fur coat?'

'If you want one.'

'Of course I don't, silly.'

'What then? Let me give you something.'

She lifted her arm and the bracelet glittered on her wrist. 'Give me something for this.'

'Certainly. What would you like?'

'Get me a fish.'

'A fish?'

'You caught me. I'm a fish. And we're by a stream. I expect there are fish in it. All symbolic.'

'A fish it shall be.'

But it was he who was the fish.

TWO

Having hooked him she began to play him, and play him up. She would arrive late at their rendezvous and find him in a wretched state of anxiety.

'I thought you weren't coming.'

'I got delayed. And I've got to get back early so let's just have a quick drink.'

'But I've come all the way . . .'

'If it's too much trouble' – spoken haughtily.

'No. Not too much trouble.'

'Don't make a fuss then.'

'Hello? Ambrose?'

'Yes. Speaking.'

'I shan't be able to make it tomorrow.'

'You won't be able to make it.'

'That's what I said.'

'But when shall we meet?'

'I might manage next Thursday. Tomorrow week.'

'Please – try to make it.'

'All right. And I'll try not to be late. Bye.'

'Deirdre?'

No reply. She had rung off.

But, just when he thought the affair was doomed to end in snatched meetings and cancelled dates, she would give him recompense.

'Here? In the car?'

'No-one's looking, silly. And no-one's likely to come. The doors are locked, aren't they?'

'Yes, but . . .'

'Of course, if you don't want me . . .'

'I do,' he said desperately.

'And I want you,' she replied softly. 'But you're right. Someone might see us. Why can't we have a night together instead of always meeting like this?'

'Would you like that?'

'For a lawyer, Ambrose, there are some things you don't catch on to very fast.'

'All right. I think I can arrange it. Next time we'll spend the night together.'

'Oh, darling.' Her arms round his neck. 'Let's get into the back. More room.'

'You mean?'

'Let's risk it.'

The dining room of a hotel in Colchester.

'It's all right, is it?' he asked. 'Being away for the night?'

She gave him a cool look. 'William thinks I'm visiting my kids.' After a pause, she added, 'I wish you wouldn't mention things like that. It makes it seem sordid.'

'I'm sorry.'

'Don't do it again.'

Later. A bedroom in the same hotel.

Halfway through undressing, standing in her underclothes, she looked across at him as he carefully folded his trousers.

'Ambrose?'

'Yes.'

'What would you do if I slapped your face?'

He dropped the trousers in an untidy heap. 'What!'

'You heard.' She moved sinuously towards him, as if her motion had its propulsion in her swaying buttocks. Lifting her right arm she brought it down swiftly so that the palm of her hand hit his left cheek hard. He recoiled under the blow, his eyes watered and his mouth sagged in shock.

'That's punishment for making me think about William earlier,' she said. 'Now kiss my hand.'

She held out the hand which had struck him.

His face was twisted with indecision and pain but after a moment's uncertainty he lowered his head and kissed her hand with a sort of subdued reverence as if she were a queen and he a humble subject.

He didn't see the smile of triumph flitting across her face. 'Tonight,' she said, 'you are going to do as I say and do exactly what I want. You understand?'

'Yes.'

'It's my pleasure, not yours, which is important.'

Nobody had ever spoken to him like this before. He could only nod his head like a bewildered servant in the presence of a stern, unpredictable mistress.

'Now go and fold up your trousers properly, then you can finish undressing me. But you'll do it respectfully. Delicately.'

When they were in bed she initiated him into a form of sex-play he had only read about and knew by a Latin name. He was almost worn out when she ordered him to lie on his back. He obeyed with a feeling of relief. But she wasn't finished. After stimulating him to a pitch where he could be used in the way she wished she climbed on top of him and straddled his thighs.

When her purpose was accomplished and they were lying side by side, entwined in each other's arms, he said, with awe in his voice, 'Never dreamed it could be like that. I was bewitched.'

'Bitched more likely,' she said with a low laugh. 'But bewitched will do. I am a witch, didn't you know?'

'I might have guessed it.'

'That can be your next present to me. A little witch on a broomstick.'

98

'I had a job finding a fish. I didn't see any witches on broomsticks.'

'Then have one made.'

'But . . . Yes. Should be possible.'

'Good. Now turn out the light and go to sleep.'

It was while the affair was at its height that Rodney telephoned one day for an urgent appointment. There was a note of desperation in his voice and Ambrose agreed to see him immediately.

Once the door was closed and they were seated – Ambrose behind his desk, Rodney in one of the chairs used by clients – Ambrose asked, 'What's the matter? Are you in some sort of trouble?'

'Yes. I am.'

'Tell me about it.'

'It's a debt. I owe money.'

Ambrose reached for propelling pencil and notepad. 'How much and what for?'

'Just under three thousand . . . I can raise the wind, given time, but the man I owe it to is threatening to tell my managing director about it unless I pay up by midday tomorrow.'

'How was this debt incurred?' asked Ambrose drily.

Rodney hung his head. 'I was away from home last night. Business. Stupidly got into a card game. Never done it before. I was a bit tight and didn't stop when I should.'

'Gambling debt. Unenforceable. You didn't sign anything? An IOU?'

'No, but there were witnesses and the bastard who's screwing me for fast payment knows my company has a strict rule against gambling.' Bitterly he added, 'It's a whim of our chairman of directors. You can commit adultery with impunity – you're a bit of a lad if you do; you can get into fights – shows you've got the right aggressive spirit; you can do almost anything short of murder except gamble. Rumour has it that his father was a gambler and made his mother's life hell. But the point is – if he gets to hear of it I shall be fired. It's written into my contract of service. Someone else got the sack for it a year ago and went to an industrial tribunal for unfair dismissal and lost his case. I wouldn't stand a chance.'

'You've been a fool,' said Ambrose, but it wasn't said unkindly.

'Yes.'

'Stella won't be pleased.'

Rodney grimaced. 'I know. If possible . . . I'd appreciate it if . . .'

'I didn't mention it?'

'Yes.'

Ambrose gave a nod of agreement. 'No need for me to say anything. This matter strictly between solicitor and client.'

Rodney let out a sigh of relief.

'Can you raise the wind by midday tomorrow?' asked Ambrose.

'I can try my bank manager for an increase in overdraft but what worries me is the blackmail angle. It's got to be a once and for all payment.'

'I can handle that,' said Ambrose. 'There may well be a case of demanding money with menaces. With the right pressures I'll see if we can't reach a settlement for something less than the amount due.'

Half an hour later Rodney left the office feeling optimistic. Not only was the matter in capable hands but a bond had been forged between him and his father-in-law. It was almost as if, in a peculiar way, they were now members of the same club. And yet Ambrose was no gambler.

Before leaving Rodney had said, 'If there's anything I can ever do for you, don't hesitate to call on me.'

'Thanks, but I hope it won't be necessary,' Ambrose

had replied, and he had reached out and patted Rodney's shoulder, a friendly gesture and one which had never been made before.

Ambrose asked her about the other charms, those collected before he had added his own gifts of a fish, witch on a broomstick and a St Christopher. ('I need the old fellow to protect me when we're bombing along in your car,' she had said.)

She didn't immediately answer his question about the other charms and, when she did, it seemed a *non sequitur*.

'Men are funny,' she said.

'Why do you say that?'

'They always want to hear about the others. The ones before. And either they get stupidly jealous or over-excited. William is the only man I've met who just didn't want to know and wouldn't want to know.'

It was all right for her to speak of Jameson, but not for him. This was a lesson he had been taught.

'I honestly think,' she went on, 'that for some men the best aphrodisiac is to hear about some other chap's efforts.'

'That wasn't the reason I asked about the charms,' he said stiffly.

'Wasn't it? Who do you think gave me them? Father Christmas?'

He said nothing.

'Not that I've got anything against Father Christmas. Perhaps that's my trouble. I've always been attracted to older men. A father complex, I guess.'

It was January and she had only an hour to spare. She had said, 'Let's not go anywhere special. We can just drive around for a while.' She explained that William was at home and in bed with a bad attack of influenza. She was supposedly out on a shopping expedition.

For Ambrose it was an unsatisfactory meeting. She

101

seemed to want to contradict or argue with almost everything he said and was, he felt, anxious to return home. Her perfunctory kiss on greeting had signalled her mood.

During the drive, and after a silence, she said, 'Don't look so wooden. You wouldn't have got anything today anyway. Wrong time of the month.'

He resented the implication that he was a randy old man on the make, the more so because it was partly true. Not for the first time he wondered whether the benefits of the affair (enhanced sense of living and experiencing emotions by-passed in youth) outweighed the disadvantages (tedious journeys to Suffolk, rearranged office appointments, duplicity). And yet she had only to give a chuckling laugh when he said something faintly amusing, or reach out to squeeze his hand, and he was once more a fish hopelessly hooked at the end of her line.

'This one,' she said, 'was given to me by my ex-husband. It's about the only thing he did give me. I had to buy the wedding ring.'

She indicated a miniature of Big Ben.

So, because he hadn't pursued the question of the other charms, but had dropped the subject, she had decided in her own good time to tell him. Not to press or pressurise her was another lesson he had learned.

'It was at a New Year's Eve party,' she continued. 'Someone had switched on the radio to hear the chimes of Big Ben. And round about the sixth stroke Neil said, "Marry me." That's the reason for Big Ben. This,' she touched a pair of dice, 'was from an American who made a living out of gambling. And this,' she fingered a pair of crossed swords, 'was from a fellow who said he was good at fencing. Told me he'd been in the Olympics for the Portuguese team, but the Portuguese haven't got a team, have they? As for this one,' she caressed a scorpion, 'I don't know that I should tell you about it. Do you want to hear?'

102

'I've heard enough,' he said.

'You don't want to hear more?' she asked artlessly. 'Hear about the men in my past?' She raised her wrist and shook the bracelet so that the charms, mementos of old loves, tinkled against each other. 'Are you sure you don't want to hear?'

'Quite sure.'

'You don't want to know everything about my charms? My charmed life?'

'No.'

'Better than a charmed death. Who'd want a charmed death?' She lowered her wrist. 'You're certain you don't want all the details? I'll tell you.'

'No.' His knuckle-white grip on the steering wheel looked as if he was straining to wrench it apart.

'Sorry,' she said sulkily, 'but you started it. Anyway, I wouldn't have told you about this one,' she touched the scorpion with the tip of a finger-nail. 'It's got a sting in the tail and I don't want you stung.'

He resolved there and then that she wouldn't get another charm from him. She was no better than those women who reckoned sexual conquests as scores or scalps. Her charms symbolised scalps. For a while they travelled without speaking. Eventually he said, 'We'd better turn back now. Don't want you to be late.'

'You want to get rid of me.'

'Nothing of the sort. You said you'd only got an hour.'

'I must be a big disappointment to you. No nooky.'

He clenched his teeth and a nerve twitched in his face.

'Never mind. There are other things. Companionship. Conversation. Did I tell you his sister has come to live with us?'

He unlocked his jaw. 'No.'

'Arrived last week. She was living on her own in rented rooms. She wrote him a pathetic letter and the next thing I know he's invited her to stay with us indefinitely. The idea is she'll help with the housework and be company for me when he's not in. That's a laugh. As if I need her company. The old crow. She dresses like a Victorian widow, would you believe. Black from top to toe. It was a case of hate at first sight. She can't stick me and I can't stick her. What's more she's nosey in a way William isn't. I think she's guessed something's going on. Between me and a man, I mean. She was standing near the phone when you rang last time.'

'Perhaps,' he began and broke off.

'Perhaps what?'

'I was going to say perhaps in future you should call me. Not the other way round. But it's probably not a good idea.'

'You mean your secretary might intercept and then you'd have some awkward explaining to do. My heart bleeds for you.'

Her tone was contemptuous.

The car braked suddenly, jerking her forward in her seat.

'What was that for?' she asked.

'I'm turning here. We're going back.'

'Suits me.'

A long silence. Snow had been falling lightly and he switched on the windscreen wipers. The countryside was a bleak film of white set against a murky grey sky. The stark outline of winter-bare trees added a final touch of chill desolation.

'I expect you'll be glad to get back to London,' she said at length.

He didn't answer at once. He didn't know whether to tell one truth which was, 'Yes, I shall be glad,' or to tell an equal truth which was, 'In spite of your exasperating ways I know I shall miss you and wish we were back together.'

He said, 'I don't know.'

'Poor Ambrose. I've mucked you about today, haven't I?'

He forced a laugh. 'Must admit I hadn't expected to spend our time driving around this benighted countryside.'

'Perhaps we should give it a break.'

'What?' Suddenly he found that he wanted very much to see her again and the thought of a break was almost unbearable.

'Perhaps we should give it a break,' she repeated. 'Not meet for a while.'

'Is that what you want?'

'I don't,' she said positively. 'But I thought you did. I was trying to make it easy for you.'

'I don't either.'

'Stop here,' she said.

'Stop?' He took his foot off the accelerator.

'Do as you're told,' she said in the bossy voice she usually reserved for the bedroom. 'Stop the car.'

He put his foot on the brake and pulled into the verge. When the car was stationary she leaned across and gave him a passionate kiss. 'That's something on account,' she said. 'Now you can drive on.'

Ambrose was bewildered but he started off again and narrowly missed being hit by an overtaking van.

'Christ, that was close,' she said.

'Sorry. Didn't look. Should have.'

'Thank heavens for my little St Christopher. He must approve of us. He's made sure we live to love another day.'

He looked down at her hand, now gently stroking his sleeve in a slow rhythm. The charms shone brightly against her pale wrist.

At the car park of the Cock Inn she said, 'Leave it for a week or two. We'll meet next month. And don't think any more bad thoughts.'

'What bad thoughts?'

'Bad thoughts you've been thinking about me. Don't deny it. It's been written all over your face.' She opened

105

the door. 'And take care driving back.' She leaned to one side and deftly pecked his cheek.

'I'll ring you at the beginning of next month,' he said.

He watched her walk swift-footed in new high-heeled boots, her coat rippling against the contours of her body. She unlocked her car door and slid into the driver's seat. When the engine burst into life she waved. He watched her drive away before he began the journey back to London. The saying, 'No fool like an old fool', crossed his mind and then became fixed in monotonous repetition like a mindless chant. But eventually it faded and before he reached the outskirts of London he was wishing he had made more of their meeting and was chiding himself for having allowed his disappointment to be so apparent to her.

'A boot! That's pretty. Was it specially made like my witch was?'

'Saw it in a shop actually. Remembered you had been wearing boots last time we met.'

'That's right. A touch of the Nancy Sinatras.'

He looked puzzled.

'Oh well,' she said, 'if you don't get it, I'm not going to tell you. But I'm going to put you through it tonight.'

She made good her threat and when he drove away from the motel the following morning he was by turns elated and ashamed. He was ashamed at having obeyed her outrageous and perverse demands and elated at having ultimately so powerfully asserted himself that she had been the one to whimper in an ecstasy of submission.

They had three more meetings before she broke her own self-imposed rule and telephoned him at his office. It was a brief call and if overheard by his staff would have sounded like a request from a client.

'One of William's aged aunts has died in Montrose in

106

Scotland. He and sister Laura are going up for the funeral. I expect the estate will need sorting out. Could you ring me later this morning? At about eleven?'

'Right.'

'Thanks. Bye.'

When he returned her call she said, 'If you're free it would be a great opportunity for me to come down for three or four days. William and the old crow will be away for a week.'

'You'd stay in London?' he asked.

'Yes, but you'd have to arrange it. If it's not convenient . . .'

He was typical of all successful lawyers. When he wished he could create delays which would make anyone opposing him frantic with impatience but, when it suited him, he could make up his mind with an immediacy which rivalled the fastest computer. Today was a fast action day.

'I'll arrange everything. It's the beginning of the holiday season. May have difficulty in booking in at a decent hotel. Could manage a suite of private rooms in Bayswater Road.'

He had fleetingly thought of inviting her to stay with him but as speedily dismissed the idea. A lawyer's conditioned prudence told him that such an invitation could be a first step towards a deeper commitment and he wasn't quite ready to put his relationship with Deirdre on a more permanent basis.

'You'll be able to spend time with me?' she asked, and he thought he detected a trace of disappointment in her voice. Perhaps she had expected him to say, 'Come and stay with me at my home.'

He said, 'I'll make time.'

'They're going tomorrow. By car. Daryll will drive them.'

'Daryll?'

'The new gardener. Old George had a heart attack and

107

has had to give up.'

'Will you come by car or train?'

'Train.'

'Meet you tomorrow evening at five-thirty by Smith's bookshop at Liverpool Street station. All right?'

'Right,' she replied.

Their three days together in London was the climax of their affair. He cancelled all appointments and gave his staff no reason for such an unprecedented move, and none had the temerity to ask. To one of his partners who jovially asked, 'Got seats for Wimbledon, Ambrose?' he replied, 'Don't spread it around.'

In fact, he did take her to Wimbledon to see play on one afternoon. That evening he took her to the theatre. During an interval while they were clutching drinks in an overcrowded crush bar she said suddenly, 'Do you mind if we leave when we've had our drinks?'

'Not enjoying the play or not feeling well?'

'Both. And I hate being hemmed in like this.'

'We'll go now. Give me your glass.'

Outside, while he was trying to hail a taxi she said, 'It doesn't make sense but halfway through the second act I had a most peculiar feeling. I went hot all over and felt terrible.'

A cab pulled into the kerb. When they had climbed in she continued her explanation. 'I've never felt like it before. I was almost crippled with anxiety.'

'Not on account of the play surely,' he replied. 'Didn't believe a word of it. Quite implausible.'

Described as a murder mystery, the play was about a woman whose body was found in the cellars of a stately home. It transpired that she had been secretly married to one of the characters, had been having an affair with another, and was the discarded mistress of the third.

'No, it was ridiculous,' she said. 'I'm sure it wasn't the play that made me feel queer. I don't know what it was.

Perhaps it was the heat. It was hot in there, and it's been a hot day.'

'Better now?'

'Much.' She snuggled against him. 'Thanks for being understanding.'

The theatre episode was the only slight flaw in what for Ambrose was three days of paradise. When the time came to see her off on her return journey he was close to suggesting she should leave William Jameson and come to live with him. But prudence, and a chance encounter with a fellow lawyer who button-holed him with the words, 'Ambrose, what are you doing here?' combined to frustrate his unspoken proposal.

As the train pulled away he felt a sense of loss and for the first time understood why parting should be such sweet sorrow.

It was three weeks before they met again and then it was for an interlude which had its mood set by her opening statement.

'I can't stay long. I'm sure sister Laura suspects something. I had a hell of a job cooking up a convincing story to get away. The old crow shadows me everywhere. It's getting to the stage where either she'll have to go or I will.'

He realised later that she was giving him the opportunity to suggest she come to live in London.

He said, 'Was it that bad?'

'Every bit as bad. And that idiot gardener doesn't make things any better.'

'The new man? What's his name?'

'Daryll. He's a fool. All right, so he can drive a car and he can dig like a mechanical excavator but I doubt if he can tell parsley from a parsnip. And he can't take his eyes off me. William doesn't seem to mind the ogling, but I do. I've had to give up sun-bathing.'

'We'll just drive around for a while.'

'Yes, please.'

He put the car into gear and they moved off.

'How old is Daryll?' he asked.

'Two years younger than me, I think.'

'A fit young fellow?'

'Beefcake. Good-looking, I suppose, in a blue-eyed, ruddy faced, mop of black curly hair, gipsy way.'

'Maybe he's read Lady Chatterley and has ideas.'

'Comic strips are his reading matter.'

'At least I don't have a serious rival,' he joked.

'Don't start that. I'm not in the mood today.'

'How did the funeral go?' he asked after a pause.

'I got back just in time. They came home earlier than expected. The old crow noticed at once that most of the windows were still closed and the rooms smelled stale. I said I'd spent most of my time out of doors and hadn't bothered with opening and shutting windows. She gave William a significant look. She's got a wonderful significant look. The "I could speak volumes if you'd let me" look.'

'Sorry to hear it. Must have spoiled our little holiday together.'

'One of those things. How about you? Everything all right?'

'Fine. Established that I'd had three days of hell with a wicked stomach bug. Spent most of my time in a darkened bedroom.'

She laughed. 'The last bit was partly true, at least.'

'Best lies always have a coating of truth. Lawyer's job sometimes to make the coating armour-plated.'

'I've got an idea. Let's go to the place where we had that first picnic.'

'You've got the time?'

'For a quick stroll, nothing more.'

But when they arrived at Santer's Wood clouds which had been threatening rain unleashed their burden and he turned the car and set off back to the Cock Inn.

110

She now became inexplicably quiet. His clipped utterances were met with equally sparse replies. He wondered whether he had said something to upset her but knew better than to ask. He was a late-starter but a quick learner and he had learned that it irritated her – unless they were playing bedroom games – to ask if he'd said or done anything wrong.

It was an unsatisfactory meeting. When she drove away from the car park she didn't turn and wave as usual. He was left feeling disquieted and vaguely annoyed. On the drive to London his annoyance increased. By the time he reached his office to spend a final couple of hours at his desk he was angry. I'm nothing more than a puppet, he thought. A puppet to be picked up or put down as the whim takes her.

Their next meeting came after two postponements which she had engineered. It was November when they did meet and she seemed in the same frame of mind as when he had last seen her.

'I'm sorry about this,' she said as she settled into the passenger seat, 'but two minutes before I left William told me he'd invited someone to dinner this evening. He's a herbalist and fascinated by William's work. William had forgotten to mention it to me before. He apologised very nicely but it means I've got to get back. I can't have an evening off.'

'I thought . . .' he began and choked off the rest of the sentence.

'You thought you were going to get your oats. Sorry to frustrate you.'

He was shaken by the crude accuracy of her assessment. Surprise and shock were replaced by cold, bottled-up fury.

'Charmingly elegant way of putting it,' he said. 'Happens to be quite wrong but the turn of phrase is poetic in its simplicity.'

She opened the car door. 'Thanks for the ride,' she said.

They hadn't even moved out of the car park.

He watched her hurrying to her car.

'Deirdre,' he called.

She didn't stop. She climbed into her car after fumbling and dropping the keys. Then she gunned the engine as though she wanted to blast off to the moon and shot out of the car park.

They didn't communicate for three months.

He broke the silence.

His mouth was dry with nerves as he said, 'It's very late, I know, but Happy New Year.'

'Thanks. And you.' She sounded formally polite.

Humbly he said, 'I'd like to meet you again.'

A very long pause. 'All right. You may. But I hope you'll be in a better mood this time.'

He swallowed hard. 'When will you be free?'

'Next Thursday.'

'Usual place and time?'

'I suppose so. Yes, all right. Must go. Bye.'

The line went dead.

He shook his head and replaced the phone.

She had sounded so uninterested that he wondered whether she would keep the date. But, unusually, she was in the car park waiting for him.

When she got into his car she offered her lips for a kiss. He sensed that everything was going to be all right.

'I can't spend the whole night with you,' she said, 'but I've worked it so that I'm free till ten.'

'You sound like a prisoner.'

'I shall end by killing that woman.'

'What would you like to do?'

'Oh, you decide. Anything goes. I couldn't care less.'

'That place – the Cross Keys – we liked it there. I could get a room.'

'Sure. Go ahead.'

Five hours later he achieved the culmination of his sexual desires but as he lay beside her he knew she had been nowhere near a climax. As a quick learner he knew better than to say something like 'Was it good for you too?' Instead, he said, 'Thank you.'

This was no less a mistake.

'Don't thank me,' she said. 'Thanks have nothing to do with it.' She rolled off the bed and began dressing. 'Just time for the obligatory coffee and brandy,' she said.

'Deirdre . . .'

'Deirdre,' she mimicked.

He felt miserable. He looked miserable.

'What's the matter?' she asked, zipping up her skirt. 'Got post-coital tristesse, have we?'

He flinched.

'That wasn't very nice of me,' she said, 'but I've been so on edge lately. William's noticed. He's given me some little red pills. They've got valerian, motherwort, wild lettuce, and God knows what in them. They're supposed to soothe the nerves.'

He went across the room to where his coat was hanging. 'I've got a little something for you.'

He handed her a small box.

She lifted the lid and parted a fluff of cotton wool to reveal a tiny charm. 'What is it, Ambrose?'

'A Lincolnshire Imp. I grew up in Lincoln and we had a door-knocker like that.'

'He's nice. Why has he only got one leg?'

'I don't know.'

'Was it specially made for me?'

'Yes.'

'That's sweet. I'm sorry I've been such a bitch. But you don't know what it's like at home. I can't move without her appearing from nowhere.'

She was no longer a beautiful, manipulative mistress in control of every situation but a despairing young woman who reminded him of his daughter and how she

113

had looked when told her baby was stillborn. His heart went out to her. He forgot past disappointments and said, 'You could come to London. Stay with me.'

Speaking with her head averted she said, 'It wouldn't work. We both know that. I'm not the right consort for a senior partner in a firm of lawyers. But thanks all the same.' She turned to face him. 'There's nothing you can do about it. It's up to me to look after myself. It always has been.'

'If there is anything . . .'

'There isn't,' she replied flatly. 'Let's change the subject, shall we.'

She was once again in control of herself and the situation.

Their next meeting was fixed for Thursday, the twenty-fifth of April.

THREE

Ambrose slept badly the night before he was due to meet her but as he drove through the north-eastern suburbs of London his misgivings faded. It was a bright spring morning and he was looking forward to seeing her again. They hadn't communicated since the last meeting three weeks earlier. She had asked him not to telephone except in emergency. 'Whenever the phone rings the old crow races to try and answer it before me,' she had explained.

It was while changing gear at a roundabout that he first realised a fault had developed in the gear-box. Within five miles he was unable to engage any gear except second. He limped to a roadside garage which was little more than a filling station. The attendant told him there was no chance of the car being serviceable until a new gear-box had been fitted and this was a major job. He would have to arrange for the car to be taken to a garage capable of undertaking the necessary work. In the meanwhile he was welcome to leave it at the side of the forecourt.

Ambrose was in a quandary. He could either call up Deirdre to cancel their date and hope she hadn't already left for their rendezvous, or he could try to hire a car. He decided to hire but when he asked the attendant if a car was available he was told, 'Sorry, we don't do car hire. You'll have to go to Romford for that.'

It was then he remembered that on most Thursdays Rodney was at his company's headquarters in Romford.

The town was only three miles away. Using a phone in the filling station's front office he put a call through. Luckily he contacted Rodney almost at once and with characteristic brevity explained what had happened. He finished, 'Not only a damn nuisance but I've got an appointment near Ipswich I don't want to miss. Shall have to hire a car. Can you recommend anyone?'

Rodney's reaction was immediate. 'No need for you to hire. You can borrow my car. I shan't be needing it till this evening. I'll send someone in it to pick you up, you can drop him back here, have your appointment and call for me on the way back. While you're away I'll arrange for your car to be picked up and taken for repair. Sorry I can't deliver the car myself but I'm very tied up.'

'Very kind of you. Most grateful.'

As a result of Rodney's co-operation he was able to reach the Cock Inn ten minutes before the meeting arranged for noon. For a few minutes he sat inside the car and then, realising she wouldn't recognise it, he got out. From time to time he paced to the car park's entrance and looked down the road. At the best of times he disliked being kept waiting, and this wasn't the best of times; he became increasingly impatient. What exasperated him was that she knew very well he was impatient by nature and he suspected that sometimes she deliberately kept him waiting. In a curious way the more she set his nerves on edge the more valuable their time together seemed and the more he needed the reassurance that she still cared about him. His frustration was increased by knowing it would be useless to reproach her for a late arrival. If he did, she would punish him by becoming cool and off-hand. She would let him know she was doing him a favour by coming; if he couldn't accept her unpunctuality he would have to lump it. 'You must take me as I am or not at all,' she had once said.

Other cars arrived and their occupants went into the pub but there was no sign of her. She was forty minutes

116

overdue. In two minutes time it would be his longest wait. The minutes ticked by; a new record for waiting was established. He had nothing to read, no distractions such as a crossword puzzle to occupy his mind, he had simply to continue waiting.

He was sick of the sight of a creosoted post supporting a large wrought-iron cockerel which swayed and creaked slightly in the breeze. He was fed up gazing at the pub's wall with its weathered red brick and four casement windows. He knew exactly the shape of the beech tree which shaded a corner of the car-park and could have drawn every branch, and almost every twig, from memory.

And still he waited.

It was three minutes past one. He climbed back into the car and slammed the door shut. A moment later he saw her drive in, slow down and look around for him.

He got out but before he reached her she was already out of her car and hurrying towards him.

'Sorry I'm late,' she said. 'I've had a hell of a morning.' And then, 'Where's your car?'

'This is it. Borrowed for the day. Mine broke down.' He opened the passenger door for her.

'It'll be a short drive around today,' she announced.

'That'll suit me. We've lost an hour anyway.'

'I've said I'm sorry.'

He noticed that she wasn't wearing her boots today but green flat-heeled shoes. These, with her sweater, suede jacket and tweed skirt gave the impression of someone dressed for a brisk walk in the country. Instead of nylon stockings she wore green woollen tights. It was obvious she intended it to be a friend day rather than a mistress day.

'Where would you like to go?' he asked, once they were on the road.

'Let's go to that little wood.'

'If you like.'

117

'It's private there.'

He nodded agreement. 'How have things been?'

'Terrible.'

'Why's that?'

'It's a war of nerves. She's like some evil bird waiting to pounce. Yesterday I screamed at her for God's sake to keep her distance.'

'What did she say?'

'She gave a twisted smile, more like a sneer, and said one day I'd be sorry.'

'What did that mean?'

'I didn't bother to ask. I went out for a while. This morning was even worse. We had a terrible row just when I wanted to get ready to leave. That's why I was late. She tried to lecture me on immorality. She didn't even let up when I was going. Followed me out to the car accusing me of every sin in the book. I couldn't get away fast enough.' She gave a harsh laugh. 'Almost ran the old crow down. Wish I had.'

'But doesn't, er, William, do anything about it? He must know the two of you don't get on.'

'Don't get on? We hate each other.'

'But doesn't he –'

'No, he doesn't,' she interrupted without waiting to hear the end of Ambrose's sentence. And then, more quietly, 'It can't go on.'

'No,' he agreed. 'Something must be done.'

She turned towards him. 'When I said it can't go on, I meant us. We can't go on. It's over, Ambrose.'

In his years as a lawyer he had sometimes come across cases in which one partner in a marriage had ignored signs from the other partner that the marriage was finished. It had always surprised him that although these signs were visible to everyone else, the innocent (or ignorant) partner was invariably shocked by revelation when revelation was inescapable. Now he was in the position of innocent (or ignorant) partner and

118

although there had been signs and signals in the past that the affair could be on its way out these had always been erased by memories of happy times or fabricated excuses for her indifferent behaviour.

Her 'It's over, Ambrose,' was like a swordthrust to his vitals; he actually felt pain in his stomach and this was followed by a sort of sinking ache as if his bruised guts had shifted to the base of his body. Mentally he was as numbed as any of his innocent clients had been when their ignorance was shattered. Sometimes with strained faces they would ask for his advice and he would side-step responsibility for interfering with what might in the long run be the best course for all concerned and he would suggest, if this had not already been tried, consultation with a marriage guidance counsellor. In his grave family lawyer manner he would say, 'Reconciliation should always be attempted and if it doesn't succeed, well, time is a great healer.'

His own trite advice now mocked him. Reconciliation must be attempted and if it failed then time would ultimately heal the wound of parting. Sensible advice, reasonable appreciation of the inevitable, logical conclusions drawn from inescapable facts, were no better than broken matchsticks when it came to the crunch.

'You do understand?' she asked and her voice had a hopeful note.

'No, I don't understand. Are you saying that because an old woman makes you feel persecuted we must give in to her pressure?'

'She's not just any old woman. She's William's sister.'

Now was the time to plead for mitigation of sentence, to employ forensic skills, not to treat her as a witness for the prosecution who must be rigorously cross-examined.

'My turn to say sorry. Haven't been understanding enough. But I do understand. Must be hellish for you. Perhaps it would be a good idea not to meet for a while.'

'No, Ambrose. I'm not talking about a temporary

119

break. This is it. The end. The reason I was so late today wasn't only on account of a row with the old crow, I was steeling myself to say it's all over.'

'I see. Look, it's difficult for me to get to grips with this and drive. Can we hold it over until we've reached the wood? We can talk about it better there.'

'There's nothing to talk about.'

'I'm not going to try to talk you out of anything, but I do want a few moments in a quiet place. The condemned man's last request.'

She took long enough to reply. 'All right,' she said grudgingly.

He drove the car on to a grassy verge by the side of a winding lane. To the left was the edge of Santer's Wood and ahead, across a field, was a fringe of trees in the first fresh green leaf of spring. When he cut the engine it was possible to hear the faint thrum of traffic on the main road and in the distance the croo-croo call of a wood pigeon sang through the still air.

'I've made up my mind,' she said.

'Can't blame you, I suppose. Never pretended to be the world's greatest lover, but I do love you.'

'Emotional blackmail,' she muttered.

'Nothing of the sort. The bare facts. Can't deny I'm shaken. I am. Is it something I've done, or haven't done?'

'Neither,' she said in a weary voice. 'It's all down to me. My fault. I've valued your friendship, I really have, but we can't go on. It's as simple as that.'

He put out his hand as if to rest it on her thigh, thought better of the gesture, and withdrew.

'It's meant a lot to me. A hell of a lot,' he added with unusual vehemence. 'Until you came along . . .' He broke off as if the sentence was too painful to complete.

'I'm sorry. Believe me, I am sorry.'

'Won't you tell me the reason?'

'Reason for what?'

120

'Reason why you want to end it.'

'Isn't it obvious?'

'Not much good at guessing. Intuition. I'm the sort of chap who needs this sort of thing spelled out. Been dealing in facts, reason, logic, too long for it to be otherwise.'

'Poor Ambrose, you make your life sound sort of – thin.'

'It was pretty thin, although I didn't realise it, before I met you.'

'And now I'm leaving you.'

He gave her a quick look but she was staring straight ahead and he couldn't tell whether she was regretful or pleased. There had been a note of satisfaction, almost smugness, in her voice.

'Yes, you're leaving me. But why? I can't believe it's because of harassment by an old woman. Don't you think I'm entitled to an explanation?'

She gave a short laugh. 'You once told me there were no rights or entitlements except those established as legal rights. Anything else was emotional and not a right. But I'll tell you all the same.' She turned and for the first time since they had stopped she looked at him fully. Her face showed no sign of stress or strain; she looked serenely smooth as a contented cat. 'It's guilt. A guilty conscience.' Then the serenity vanished. 'That old crow has been whispering, putting it into William's mind that I'm a loose woman who doesn't give a damn for his feelings. He doesn't say anything but he gives such sorrowful looks. I feel awful. If it wasn't that he was a good man, a kind man, perhaps it wouldn't get to me. But it does. I feel a heel.'

'Does he know about us? You and me?'

'He knows there's someone, but he doesn't know who.'

'Nobody knows?'

'Nobody. I'm not the kiss and tell sort.' She paused.

121

'He wants to marry me.'

'Do you want to marry him?'

'I don't know. I honestly don't. And now you've been given your precious reason can we leave? I want to get back.'

He didn't move.

'I want to get back, Ambrose.'

'Not yet. Don't understand why we can't meet even if it's only once or twice a year. Just for a drink and a chat.'

She shook her head. 'It's got to be a clean break. Nothing else works.'

'Your experience?'

'Yes, if you like. My experience.' She sounded defiant.

'Experience of breaks, clean and otherwise?'

She faced him angrily. 'Yes, yes, yes. Plenty of experience if that's what you want to hear.'

His own anger was rising. The resolution not to be a cross-examining lawyer was forgotten. 'Plenty of experience. I can believe that. You must have found my efforts laughably naive.'

'Don't push it. You might hear the truth. Let's leave on a civilised note.'

'Laughably naive,' he repeated. 'Ridiculously naive for a man of my age.'

'Cut it out,' she said harshly.

'You must let me have my say. You've had yours. I've heard about your conscience, suddenly so delicate, now you can listen to me. I've put all sorts of things at risk because of you . . .'

'Your choice,' she interrupted. 'Nothing to do with me.'

'Oh, yes it is. It takes two to make a bargain and two to break it.'

'Wrong. First, there was no bargain. And second, if there was, one can break it, and I am. Now please drive me back. I want to get home.'

'The old woman has got on your nerves and things

122

must be difficult but . . .'

'No buts. Take me back. I've had enough of this.'

'No, you can wait a bit longer. God knows I've often waited long enough for you. How do you think I felt today? And there have been other times.'

'You're wasting your breath, Ambrose.'

Wasting his breath! The phrase echoing across the years whipped his anger into fury. Who was she to tell him he was wasting his breath!

'I treated you like a princess but you're nothing but a . . .' He checked himself just in time.

She raised an eyebrow. 'Whore?' she enquired.

'I didn't say that.'

'You meant it. And if that's what you want to think, feel free. I couldn't care less. And now if you don't take me back this minute I'm leaving.'

'You can't leave.'

'Oh, can't I? I can walk to the road and thumb a lift. I'll pull up my skirt and show off my legs and hope I get a randy young man.'

She was quietly opening the door as she spoke.

'Don't be a fool,' he cried, reaching out. But she eluded his grasp and was out of the car before he could stop her.

As she started running towards the main road his fury peaked into a violent desire to hurt her.

FOUR

When he saw his father-in-law leaning against a pillar in the reception area Rodney was so taken aback he paused in his stride. The older man's body seemed to have shrunk within his overcoat but the ghostly pallor of his face merging with the grey of his hair made his head grotesquely large and he gave the impression of a hydrocephalic cadaver which has been propped upright. Rodney hurried across a polished tile floor. 'Are you feeling all right, old man?' He had never before called Ambrose by this familiar term but it came out spontaneously.

'Don't feel so good.'

'Come along. I'll take you to the rest room. Would you like a cup of tea?'

Ambrose's face was haggard and his eyes sunken. 'A glass of water would be fine.'

They went to a large room which could have been an airport lounge with its clouded glass walls, chrome and rexine chairs and low tables of laminated teak. When they were seated Rodney said, 'Now tell me what's happened. Have you been in an accident?' He hesitated. 'Is the car okay?'

Ambrose managed a twitch of the lips, meant to pass as a smile. 'Don't worry. The car's in one piece.'

'Do you need a doctor?'

The older man shook his head, and with a visible effort pulled himself together, straightening his back and squaring his shoulders. Colour was returning to his cheeks. 'You'd better know,' he said.

Apart from two young girls reading magazines in a far corner the room was empty. Nevertheless, Rodney had to move close to catch what Ambrose was saying.

'I've been a fool. No fool like an old fool they say, and it's true. Fell for a young woman. Been seeing her on and off for quite a while.' He paused for so long Rodney felt obliged to prompt.

'That's where you were going today? To see her? She lives somewhere near Ipswich?'

'Thereabouts.'

Rodney hazarded a guess. 'And it's all over?'

'All over. I'll say it's all over.'

'Is she . . . trying to blackmail you?'

Ambrose closed his eyes. 'She's dead.'

One of the girls laughed. 'Read this,' she said to her friend. 'It's funny.'

Ambrose seemed oblivious to their presence. Without preamble he went into an account of how he had met Deirdre, hoping for a pleasant afternoon with her, only to find that so far as she was concerned this was to be the final meeting.

'We sat in the car and she told me coolly it was all over. She had a guilty conscience and it was goodbye. There was more, but that's the essence. Shook me badly. Tried to persuade her to reconsider. Had no effect. I'm sorry to say I began to lose my temper. Felt I'd been used and then chucked aside when I was no further use. I suppose you could say we were beginning to quarrel but it didn't get that far. She flung open the door and ran off to the main road. Said she was going to thumb a lift or something like that. I was furious. Can't remember ever having been so furious. Even had a red mist in front of my eyes.'

Ambrose fell silent and breathed heavily. Rodney, fearful that he might have a heart attack, asked

125

anxiously, 'Are you sure you're all right? I could get a doctor.'

'No need. Just ordering my thoughts. Have to get events in proper sequence.'

'What events?'

'She ran off down the lane. A minute later, maybe two minutes, I heard a scream. A woman's scream. It came from the direction she'd taken. Didn't do anything. Very, very ashamed to admit it, but I thought if she's in trouble it's her own damn fault. Anyway, I was still in no fit state. Hands shaking. Another minute, maybe two or three, passed, and I felt back to normal. Started the car. Had a job turning it but managed to. Hasn't got power steering like mine. Drove slowly down the lane looking around in case she was still about. Honestly didn't expect to see her. Imagined she would have reached the main road and if she hadn't been picked up I would have given her a lift. But just past a bend in the lane, right by a dense part of the wood, saw her, half-hidden by a bush, lying on her back. Jumped out of the car and caught sight of a man plunging through the wood. Couldn't describe him. Just a fleeting glimpse. Went over to Deirdre. Dead.' Ambrose covered his face with his hands. 'It was terrible,' he whispered.

'My God! You've reported it?'

'No. I panicked. Thought I could be accused. End my career. Everything. Best thing would be to clear off fast. Pulled her body so that it was completely out of sight from the lane and ran back to the car. Drove down here intending to call the police, anonymously from a call-box. Would say I was someone out for a walk and had seen a body. Tell them where and ring off.'

'And have you?'

'Couldn't bring myself to.'

'The man she lived with doesn't know about you, does he?'

'Don't think so.'

126

'Then there's no reason why you should be suspected of anything.'

Ambrose didn't reply immediately. He seemed to have some difficulty in breathing. In the space of an afternoon a healthy man in late middle-age had become sick and very old.

The two girls who had been reading magazines, got up and left the room, their shoe-heels clicking noisily on the tiled floor.

Ambrose's breathing became more regular. 'There's a reason why I might be suspected,' he said. 'Good reason.'

'Why? No-one need know you were in that area. I shan't tell anyone. I can keep quiet about you borrowing my car. The guy who delivered it to you hasn't a clue who you were or why you needed it. I don't see why you should be suspected.'

'I do. She was wearing a gold bracelet full of little charms. I gave her some of them. And one or two were specially made for me. They could be traced. I could be traced.'

'Was she wearing the bracelet?'

'Yes. And fool that I was, I didn't take it. It's still on her wrist.'

A young man entered the room, looked around, and walked out.

'Have you written her any letters?' Rodney asked.

'No letters. Take the advice I always give to clients. Don't put anything in writing unless you've checked it out first with your lawyer.'

'Do you know if she's told anyone about you?'

'Don't think she has. I specifically asked. She said nobody knew. She wasn't the kiss and tell sort, she said.'

'So it's only the bracelet which could link you with her. In that case all you have to do is go back, take off the bracelet, and you should be in the clear.'

'Don't think I could face going back.'

Rodney patted the old man's shoulder. 'Don't worry. I'll drive. We'll go together.'

'You'll come with me?' A note of hope instead of the monotone of despair vibrated in Ambrose's voice.

'I'll come with you. But first I'll have to call Stella. I'll tell her I'm being kept at a conference and shan't be home till very late. It's happened before. What about you? Do you need to call anyone?'

'No.'

'Good. You stay here, I'll make my call, and then we'll drive up there.'

As the car raced north along a dual-carriageway, by-passing Chelmsford and Colchester, Ambrose spoke almost incessantly of his affair with Deirdre Jameson omitting only details of bedroom intimacies. It was as if the waters of speech had burst in flood through the dam of childhood inhibition and adult habit. He gave dates of meetings, verbatim reports of various conversations, and his opinions and feelings about Deirdre. Although Rodney occasionally interrupted the flow with a question, he might have been a priest listening to a garrulous but well-ordered confession or a police investigator obtaining evidence.

At one point he said, 'You have a remarkable memory. Do you keep a diary?'

'I have a secret diary, yes.'

'It had better be destroyed.'

'It will be. That's a priority.'

'This guy you saw running away,' Rodney continued. 'Could you guess his age?'

'No. He was moving fast and in shadow.'

'What was he wearing?'

'Couldn't really see. Something dark. Overcoat or raincoat.'

'It couldn't have been a woman?'

'No, don't think so. The outline and everything about

128

him seemed male.'

'Have you any idea who it could have been?'

'None. Probably a total stranger. Some fellow hanging around. A vagrant. Saw a pretty woman and attacked.'

'But nothing was taken, so far as you know, was it?'

'That's right.'

'When you drove away did you see anyone where the lane joins the main road? Could anyone have seen this car and perhaps taken its number?'

'Luckily there wasn't anybody. And no traffic. Unless someone was in hiding, watching, there wasn't a soul around.'

'That's good . . . I honestly think you needn't worry. Once we've got the bracelet there shouldn't be anything to connect you with her.'

'Hope you're right. She might have kept a diary too.'

Rodney turned down a filter from the highway and within a few minutes they were close to the lane. He slowed down to allow cars to overtake. In the darkness it wasn't easy to see the junction and they overshot. 'Never mind,' said Rodney. 'It'll be easier to turn into the lane coming from the opposite direction and a better chance of doing it when there isn't another car in sight.'

When he finally pulled in at the spot indicated by Ambrose Rodney switched off the headlights and took a torch from the glove compartment.

Deirdre's body was where Ambrose had left it. Stooping down Rodney carefully removed the bracelet and tried to hand it to his father-in-law but Ambrose started back as if he was being offered a live snake. 'No!'

Stifling the exasperation he felt, Rodney said, 'Look, we've come all the way here for just this purpose.'

Very reluctantly the older man took the bracelet and stood with it dangling from his fingers as if he was frozen to the ground.

'I've been thinking,' said Rodney, 'if we moved her a bit further into the wood the chances of her being

129

discovered will be much less.'

'Can't think straight. Damn tired.'

'In due course one of us can phone an anonymous tip-off to the police, but not immediately.'

'Yes.'

'You'll have to give me a hand with the moving.'

Ambrose remained stock-still as if paralysed by shock.

'Give me that!' Rodney took the bracelet and stuffed it in his pocket. 'I'll look after it for a while. Now, if you'll take her legs, I'll take the top half and we'll carry her towards the centre of the wood.'

'Not a big wood.'

'Just a few yards so that she's properly out of sight.' Rodney flashed his torch around. 'We're not all that far from the main road. Just past those brambles there's a clump of bushes. We'll make for that.'

'Leave it to you.'

'Come on then.'

The body was surprisingly light and when it had been concealed Rodney fetched her handbag and placed it nearby. He was still wearing driving gloves but, even so, he wiped the handle as if removing fingerprints.

'That's it. Let's get back.'

He had to assist Ambrose who was unsteady on his feet, reeling slightly as if drunk.

On the journey back to London, in contrast to his earlier behaviour, the old man was silent and spoke only when spoken to and then used a customary minimum of words.

She had said, 'I've kept a casserole in the oven, but I'm afraid it's almost dried up.'

'Don't worry. I'm not all that hungry. We had beer and sandwiches sent up.'

He looked tired. 'It's hardly worth changing,' he said, 'I'll just take off my jacket.'

As he draped the jacket over the back of a chair he

130

noticed that the top pocket was empty. It should have held his wallet. For a moment he felt as Ambrose had looked – paralysed by shock. The wallet must have worked its way out of the pocket while they were moving the body. It could be lying in the wood. When the body was discovered, the wallet would be found with its contents of credit cards and driving licence. He felt the lower pocket and his fingers touched the bracelet.

'What is it?' she asked. 'What's the matter?'

'My wallet. It's gone.'

'Perhaps you dropped it in the car.'

He rushed out to the garage. As he feared, there was no sign of the wallet. He hastily concocted a story to explain its loss. He would say his pocket must have been picked by a couple of yobbos.

They were going up to the cottage that weekend. If possible, he would stop on the way up or the way back and search. Somehow this must be managed without Stella being present. As for Deirdre, she'd have to remain unburied, her death unreported, even though this would distress Ambrose whose last words on parting had been, 'I hate to think of her lying there. We ought to call the police.' And he, Rodney, had replied, 'Leave it till the morning.' Now he would have to contact Ambrose and tell him to do nothing until the wallet was found or, at least, until he was sure he hadn't lost it in the wood.

A CHARMED DEATH
Part 3

ONE

The wedding anniversary wasn't a joyful echo of wedding bells. Disconcerted by the visit from Detective Inspector Cook Stella didn't want to work out the implications of what she'd just been told, and so she said, 'I simply don't believe you.'

'It's true.'

'It can't be. Not Dad.'

He went to the cabinet and without asking if she wanted one he poured her a drink. While there, he poured himself another.

'So that's what playing detective has done,' he said. 'Why didn't you throw that damn imp away or put it back where you found it?'

He handed her a gin and tonic, more alcohol than mixer.

'I still don't believe you. Dad isn't . . . He isn't like that.'

'Like what? He's a man. He's human.' He spoke with such vehemence it sounded as if he was God's advocate defiantly justifying the male sexual drive of the entire animal kingdom in the entire universe.

She sipped the drink, swallowed, and said, 'You've been protecting him. And all the time I thought . . .'

'You thought the worst of me.'

'I'm sorry. I don't know what to say.'

He slumped into a chair. 'The damage is done. No use crying over spilt milk.'

135

'What'll happen now?'

She, usually the one in control, believing herself to have the stronger will, was appealing to him for help.

'I don't know. The police will trace who made the charm, question him, and eventually question your father.'

'How much do you know about all this?'

'Just about everything. He bared his soul.'

'Tell me. Please tell me.'

'Tell you what?'

'Everything. I must know. When did it start? How did it start?'

'He told me in confidence when he was under stress.'

'For God's sake,' she cried. 'I'm his daughter!'

'And my wife. This is some anniversary. Let me know when you feel like eating. I'll go down to the Chinese take-away.'

'I've said I'm sorry. I really am. I can understand you must feel bitter. But please try to understand me. I've got to know . . . Did he do it?'

Rodney slowly shook his head. 'I'm sure he didn't.'

'Then who? Does he know? You said he bared his soul. When was that?'

'The night we drove up to the wood.'

She looked incredulous. 'Drove up? What's been happening?'

'I didn't want you involved in this, and nor did he.'

She came across to him. 'I am involved. You must tell me everything. Please.'

'All right.' He indicated her glass. 'Like another?'

'No, thanks.'

She sat on the arm of his chair and he slid his arm round her waist. 'I'll begin at the beginning,' he said, and for the next half hour he repeated all he could remember of Ambrose's confession about the affair, sometimes inadvertently transposing events and not always accurate on detail but substantially it was an accurate

136

account. She listened in silence. When he had finished she said, 'And to think I suspected you when all the time you were shielding him.'

'It's in the past. Forget it.'

'Thanks for doing what you did. I wish to God I hadn't taken that imp to Selkey.'

'So do I, but it's done. Maybe it won't be traced.'

'But if it is?'

'There's still no proof your father was up there the day Deirdre was killed. The worst that can happen is that he'll be put under pressure by the police and his office might hear about it. There could be gossip. He needs to have a good story ready and stick to it.'

'You must warn him.'

'I will.'

'When?'

'Tomorrow. I'll call him tomorrow.'

'No. Tonight. He must be told as soon as possible. You don't have to tell him I know.'

'Look, Stel, I've got to think this through. I'm not calling anyone until I've worked through the possibilities. It'll take the police time to track the goldsmith who made the imp. Tomorrow is soon enough.'

'If you think so.' She sounded doubtful.

'I'm sure.'

'You will warn him?'

'I'll warn him.'

She relaxed slightly. 'What a business,' she sighed. 'I wonder who could have done it.'

'It might be anyone. Some guy could have seen them in the car and spied on them. A peeping Tom. He would see her leave in a hurry, follow her and try to get fresh. She might have resisted and he might have panicked, grabbed her throat and throttled her. She did scream. He might have been trying to stop her. Realising what he'd done he ran.'

'You think it was a stranger?'

'That's my guess but who knows. It's anyone's guess.'

He switched out the light and turned towards her.

Quickly she said, 'I know it's our anniversary, darling, but . . .' The 'but', spoken with a certain emphasis, was in itself a caution, a declaration of intent, and a sentence. He understood. Sentence had been passed. It amounted to, 'No sex, please, I'm not in the mood.'

'You've had quite a day,' he said.

'Just hold me close.' She snuggled into his arms. 'That time you lost your wallet,' she ventured.

'You've guessed. When I came back from getting the bracelet I knew I must have lost it up in the wood.'

'And when we went to the cottage you hoped to find it?'

'Right. Speaking of the cottage, there's no reason why we shouldn't go there this weekend as planned.'

'Don't you think we should stay here?'

'Why?'

She had no answer.

'I'll take my clubs. I enjoy playing up there.'

A chink of light was showing between loosely drawn curtains.

'Whoever gets up first must close those curtains,' he said.

'I thought it was funny you should want to stop to give Max a walk. Usually you want to press on.'

'Is that why you came with me? Because you thought it was unusual?'

'Not really. I don't think so.'

'Trouble was you came on me so suddenly. I'd just picked up the wallet and you were right behind me. I knew you'd see Deirdre so I pretended Max had found her.'

'Max hasn't got much of a sense of smell,' she pointed out.

'True. But I didn't think of that at the time.'

A silence broken by an aeroplane flying overhead. As its sound diminished she said, 'I've been thinking,' and she waited for him to say, 'Thinking what?'

He obliged her.

'About Mr Jameson,' she said. 'Could it have been him?'

'I haven't a clue. But I'll bet the police put him under pressure . . . He must have been incredibly broad-minded.'

'I've got a confession to make,' she announced.

'Confession? I'll warn you I'm not that sort of broad-minded.'

'Not that sort of confession, silly.'

She went on to tell him of her visit to William Jameson, and finished, 'It's been preying on my mind. I can't seem to think of anything else. It's, well, almost an obsession.'

'He's hired a private detective, you say. Obviously he wants to find the killer.'

'That's what I thought. But perhaps it's just a cover to take suspicion away from himself.'

'You might have something there. Complaisant lover who was secretly very jealous.'

'How many of those things did Dad give her? Do you know?'

'He didn't say. But quite a few.'

'Poor old Dad. He reckons he's good at summing up people but he certainly made a mistake with her.'

'We all make mistakes,' he said, so quietly it was almost inaudible.

The last words she spoke to him before he left for work the following morning were, 'Don't forget to ring Dad.'

Almost the first words she spoke on his return that evening were, 'Did you call Dad?'

'I called, yes. But he was out at court.'

Her face fell. 'Didn't you call again?'

'I meant to, but got sidetracked.'

139

'So he doesn't know about the imp?'

'Not yet. I'll ring again tomorrow.'

'Do it tonight.'

His jaw muscles tightened and his face hardened. 'Tomorrow will do. It won't be that easy for the police to trace the goldsmith.'

'I don't see why not. They could have done it today. I wish you'd let him know. He should be warned.'

'Look, even if the police did ask about it before I can tell him he'd manage perfectly well. He's a lawyer.'

She shook her head, perplexed. 'You seem so casual about it. It could be very awkward for him. Asked to explain how something he had specially made came to be on the bracelet of a murdered woman. It would be obvious he'd been a lover.'

'Not obvious at all. They were tokens of esteem, nothing more. Small gifts from a respected and respectable elderly admirer.'

'Rubbish,' she retorted.

'If that's how you feel there doesn't seem any point in carrying on this boring conversation.'

The evening ahead was effectively ruined by this interchange. During their meal long silences were punctuated by coldly polite small talk. When the dishes were cleared away he said, 'I've got paperwork to catch up on,' and disappeared.

She slept badly and woke on a nightmare in which she was trying to find the court where her father was being tried for murder. She knew that if she could get there and explain to the judge that he couldn't possibly have killed Deirdre her father would be acquitted but nobody could tell her exactly where the court-house was and suddenly she was in a building she didn't recognise, but it was some sort of prison, and she saw her father being hustled along a corridor by a warder. A metal grille prevented her from running to him and when she tried to shout to attract attention no sound came from her mouth.

Instinctively, and seeking comfort, she clasped Rodney. He responded by rolling on top of her and pressing his mouth against hers. She managed to tear herself away. 'I've just had a nightmare,' she said indignantly.

'Thanks! Thanks very much! Sorry to be a nightmare!'

He removed himself to the furthest edge of the bed and turned his back.

They didn't speak at breakfast but as he was leaving she said, 'You will phone Dad, won't you?'

'I said I would, didn't I?' Without waiting for her reply he walked out of the house.

TWO

Shortly before midday she made a decision. She would telephone her father to check whether Rodney had called him. As she lifted the phone and began dialling she thought, Am I getting neurotic about this?, but it didn't stop her.

When she was put through she said, 'Hello Dad. It's me. Are you busy?'

'Hello Stella. I'm always busy.' It was said gently.

'Has Rodney rung you?'

'Rodney? No. Why?'

'He tried yesterday but you were in court.'

The line went so silent she thought they had been disconnected. 'Hello,' she said anxiously.

'I wasn't in court yesterday,' said Ambrose.

'Were you in all day?'

'These are strange questions, Stella.'

'I'm sorry, Dad, but were you in the office all day? Could Rodney have got through to you?'

'Certainly.'

'Oh, God,' she murmured.

'What's that?'

'Nothing. I don't suppose it's possible, but if I came up to town straight away you wouldn't be free, would you?'

'I could be. What is it?'

'I just want to see you. To talk. I'll be at the office within the hour.'

'Good. We'll have lunch. I've been meaning to ask

when you planned to come up.'

'Be seeing you then,' she said.

On her way to central London she made an effort to grip something her imagination had shied from – her father in the role of lover to an attractive woman much younger than himself. To her, her own parents had been curiously asexual; they were somehow immune from primitive urges. As a topic of conversation, sex had never been mentioned in the household and although she had always been very fond of her father, and when young had held him in some awe, she couldn't recall ever being troubled by incestuous longings.

How was she going to get across to him that not only did she know he must have had an affair with Deirdre Jameson but also that he could be subjected to some severe police enquiries? Obviously she would have to reveal that Rodney had told her if there was no way of avoiding it.

Troubled by thoughts she almost missed getting out of the train at the station nearest his office and just managed to scramble through the automatic doors before they closed. She was still undecided how to broach the subject of Deirdre. For many, it would have been easy enough to speak directly but for a woman with a sheltered upbringing whose parents had never discussed the so-called facts of life with her, had never once told the mildest of risqué jokes, never indeed acknowledged that reproductive processes existed, it was difficult to confront her father with the bald statement that the police had possession of something he had given his murdered mistress.

He took her to a restaurant near his office where fish was a speciality and the walls were hung with nets and a huge stuffed pike in a glass case had a place of honour in a small anteroom which served as a bar.

'How about something before we order?' he said.

'That would be nice. A dry sherry.'

'Two dry sherries please,' he said to the waiter and, turning to her, 'this is an unexpected pleasure. Everything all right at home, I hope.'

'Oh, yes.'

'Rodney fit and well?'

'He was when he left this morning,' she said smiling brightly to disguise what she really felt about Rodney's brusque exit earlier in the day.

'And so to what do I owe this pleasure?' he asked.

She might have guessed that he would come straight to the point, even if she hadn't the nerve.

She gazed unhappily at the stuffed pike and it flashed into her mind that she might be able to make something of the symbolism of fish and from this lead to the fish charm on the bracelet, but she couldn't find the right words. She couldn't say, 'Looking at that pike it occurs to me that fish make interesting symbols.'

'Take your time,' he said quietly. 'There's no hurry. Any holiday plans?'

Grateful for this diversion she said, 'Nothing special. We're going up to the cottage tonight and coming back late Sunday.'

'Hope the weather holds.'

'So do I. You must come up some time, Dad. We'd love to have you.'

'I know. Never seem to have weekends free. Overworked and understaffed.'

She looked at him fully almost for the first time since they'd met. 'You don't seem to be suffering. I suspect you're a workaholic.'

As she spoke she noted that his face and forehead were remarkably unlined for a man of his age and although his hair was grey and his nose seemed to have thickened slightly she realised he wasn't a bad looking man. She lowered her eyes lest he guess she was seeing him in an entirely new light, as a lover and not as dear old

144

Dad whose whole existence was sealed in by legal textbooks and clients' problems, and whose experience of adultery and fornication was second-hand, hearsay.

'That's an evil fish,' she said nodding towards the pike. 'I'll bet there were a lot of little fish who offered a prayer of thanks when he got caught.'

'Yes, an ugly brute.'

'Talking of prayer, wasn't the fish a symbol for the early Christian church?'

'That's right. Symbolic of many things. Fish.' A fleeting sadness shadowed his eyes. He blinked, and they were clear again. 'Don't want to push you, my dear, but what brought you hotfoot to town. Was it something to do with me?'

She nodded.

The sherry arrived, and also the head waiter with two menus. The break gave her a chance to weigh alternatives. She decided she wouldn't delay the inevitable. When they were free to talk again she said, 'It's a long story, and absolutely no fault of Rodney's, who was terribly loyal to you, but I've found out about the bracelet and the charms on it, or some of them.'

If he was disconcerted it didn't show on his face. 'I don't have to ask which bracelet,' he said, 'but I'd be interested to know which charms.'

'A Lincoln Imp.'

'Ah, yes. What about a Lincolnshire Imp?'

Slowly at first but rapidly gaining confidence she told him of how Rodney's initial obsession with 'the case' had made her suspicious that he might have been involved in murder, and then, how his obsession like some contagious disease had been transferred to her and she had, as Rodney expressed it, 'played detective'. She mentioned the shaving-stick container and how the imp had been detached and she had hidden it before putting the bracelet back in the container, and how she had gone to a jeweller in the hope that he might assist in tracing the

145

charm's maker.

'After the visit from Cook,' she concluded, 'I had to tell Rodney. I made it impossible for him. I drove him into a corner. In the end he told me you'd given the imp to her.'

'Well, now that's off your chest, shall we order?' He beckoned a waiter. 'What would you like as a starter?' He continued as if they had been chatting about trivialities. It wasn't until they were seated at a table eating Dover Sole *bonne femme* (hers filleted by the waiter; his on the bone) that he said, 'You aren't worried on my behalf, are you?'

'I didn't want you to be at a disadvantage. I thought you should know the imp might be traced to you.'

'You did the right thing. Incidentally, I checked with my receptionist. She doesn't remember Rodney ringing, let alone telling him I was in court. But she wasn't on the switchboard all the time. A temp took over for an hour or so. Not that it matters.' He concentrated on prising fish from its bones. 'Terrible business. Like you, I've often wondered who could have done it. Don't recall being followed by another car, but then my mind wasn't on such things. My guess is that it'll stay unsolved.' He glanced up at her. 'Does it surprise you that your father should be mixed up in something like this?'

'To be honest, it did. That is, at first. I'd never thought of you . . .'

'As being other than a symbol for myself,' he finished for her. 'Symbol of paternity. Archetypal father figure. Odd I should be cast in that role. Never been particularly paternal or fatherly in my attitudes, but a surprising number of clients seem to see me that way, and I think Deirdre did. To some extent. Strange how people always see one as they want to see one and never as one truly is. I'd say most divorce cases I've handled have come about as a result of one party insisting, against all reason, in believing the other to be something different from what clearly they were, usually more perfect than any human

146

being could be.'

For Stella it was as though something which previously had been in black and white, and two-dimensional, was gradually changing into colour and having depth. The man seated opposite wasn't simply her father; a stereotype of whom she was fond; he was an individual with a personality as unique as his fingerprints and far more complicated than the whorls of skin on his thumb and fingertips.

Without thought for the consequences she asked, 'Did you love her?'

'Very much.'

'Did she make you happy?'

'Most of the time, yes.'

'I'm glad.'

'Mind you, I was furious sometimes. Irritating habit of keeping me waiting. On our last date I thought she'd never arrive but when she did she certainly didn't waste time.'

'How do you mean?'

'She was out of her car and running towards me as if she was being pursued by the Furies.'

'Rodney introduced you, didn't he?'

'I've often thought about that,' he said, after a pause, 'she was making a film for his product but to my knowledge they had never met before that day, and yet . . .'

'And yet?'

'I don't know. He seemed very sure of himself. As if he knew she'd come and have a meal with us. Fortuitous that he got called away and had to go to Leeds.'

She regarded him intently. 'What are you saying, Dad?'

He shook his head. 'An unworthy thought.'

'Tell me. Tell me the unworthy thought.'

'You'll think it unlikely perhaps, but it's not unknown for someone who wants to get out of a situation which

147

has become stale and unprofitable to find a successor and pass on responsibility. It's done with unremunerative contracts and failing companies, and sometimes with human relationships.'

'I don't find it unlikely. I'm not an innocent little girl any more.'

He looked at her appraisingly and in a way she had not seen before. She found his look pleasantly disturbing.

'No, you're not,' he said. 'Do you know, I hadn't realised this before, but there's something about you which reminds . . . Oh, never mind.'

She almost said, 'Reminds you of Deirdre?' but the wine waiter suddenly materialised at their table to top up their glasses and the question remained unspoken. She felt the beginnings of light-headedness. 'I shall get squiffy,' she said.

'Doesn't do any harm to let loose now and again. Only dangerous if it becomes a habit.' He gave a short laugh. 'Talking like a father-figure again. That's getting to be a bad habit.'

She picked up her glass and drank. 'Letting loose now and again sounds like good advice to me,' she said, and for a moment wished that the man seated opposite was not her father.

'What was that smile for?' he asked.

'Nothing. Just a thought that flashed through my mind. This fish is delicious.'

THREE

He took the direct route avoiding Santer's Wood.

She didn't ask whether he had remembered to call her father and he didn't volunteer the information. The coolness between them was thawing slower than usual into a watchful willingness to raise the temperature degree by degree. During the journey she pretended to doze fitfully into sleep and he didn't disturb her.

It was dusk as they travelled the last few miles to the cottage. Without warning he braked violently but not fast enough to avoid a large bird which had flown unexpectedly across their path. Stella glimpsed its laboriously flapping wings as it tried to gain height a second before it crashed into the windscreen. The car squealed to a halt. They both jumped out and ran back. A pheasant lay dead at the side of the road, its outline like a crumpled cockaded hat.

Rodney picked it up. 'It'd make a meal. What do you think?'

'It's okay by me,' she said.

'Do you know what to do?'

'Pluck and pull. I saw my grandmother do it often when I was a kid. I helped sometimes.'

They returned to the car. On arrival at the cottage he took Max for a short walk while she unpacked the few necessaries they had brought with them.

She was halfway through plucking the pheasant when he came back. 'I won't make a joke about a pheasant plucker,' he said.

'Don't. You know I don't like that word.'

Copper-red and golden brown feathers lay spread out on newspaper. The bird, stripped of its glorious plumage, looked pathetically small.

'Aren't they supposed to be hung?' he asked.

'In season, the beginning of October to the beginning of February, they should be hung for about a week. But we're out of season and I want to get it into the fridge. There should be enough breast meat on this one but a hen would have been better.'

He stood beside her, watching. 'I've never plucked a bird, but I've killed them.'

'Yes?' She looked up briefly.

'When I was a boy. Fourteen. We had a holiday at a farm in Devon. I think the farmer took a fancy to me. You sense these things. Nothing was said or done. But he showed me how to kill a chicken and let me do it.'

She continued to pluck. 'Is it easy?'

'If you have the right technique, yes. You hold them by the legs, head down. Get the back of the head in the palm of your hand and with your first and second fingers bend the head back firmly. The neckbone is parted just below the head. If it's done right, it's over in an instant.' He gave a nervous laugh. 'The first time I did it I almost . . .' He stopped.

'You what?'

'Nothing. Forget it.'

She knew intuitively that the memory associations of his first killed chicken belonged to adolescent experience, were best kept private, and might be distasteful to her. Quickly she said, 'If you want to make yourself useful you can put on the kettle for a cup of tea.'

'Sure. Are we eating tonight?'

'I'll make an omelette when I've finished this.'

'Fine.' He moved away.

'By the way,' she said, concentrating hard on her

task, 'did you phone Dad today?'

'Yes.'

'When?'

'After your lunch with him.'

She heard him plug in the kettle and flick the switch.

'You didn't mention it,' she said.

'No, and you didn't mention you'd had lunch with him.'

'I was waiting for you to say something.'

'And I was waiting for you.'

A taut silence broken by the hum of the kettle.

'What did he say?' she asked.

'That you'd had lunch together and you'd told him about the imp. It made my call superfluous.'

'I felt he ought to know.'

'You didn't trust me to tell him.'

'It wasn't that.'

'So nice to be trusted, particularly by one's wife.'

She took a deep breath, audibly, and said nothing. The kettle's hum increased. She heard him putting cups and saucers on a tray.

'Why was it necessary for you to tell him?' he asked.

'It wasn't that I didn't trust you, but you have other things on your mind. You could forget. I thought he should know as soon as possible.'

'Well, now he knows, and he knows his dear daughter knows. Great. Pity you weren't included in the first place. We could all have gone to the wood for the bloody bracelet. Had a party.'

'No need to swear.'

He laughed. 'You call that swearing.'

The kettle began to whistle. He poured the water. 'Your tea's made,' he said.

'Aren't you having any?'

'I want something stronger.' He went to the room where drinks were kept in a cupboard. When he returned, holding a glass of whisky, she had finished

151

plucking the bird and had donned rubber gloves to pull out the innards. 'Messy job,' he remarked.

Abruptly she asked, 'How well did you know Deirdre?'

'So that's on your mind, is it? What makes you think I knew her?'

'You introduced her to my father.'

'That's right. You know the circumstances. She was making a commercial. When it was finished we took her for a meal.'

'And you got called away.'

'I had to go somewhere at a moment's notice.'

'Why?'

'Something cropped up. An emergency.'

'What?'

He made an exasperated, impatient gesture. 'I don't remember exactly. A non-delivery, I think, and a customer screaming about cancelling a contract.'

The bird had been gutted and she began to wash it under the tap. The running water washed blood off her gloves and splashed pink on the stainless steel sink.

Without looking at him she said, 'That's funny. When we were having lunch Dad said you'd been called away to Leeds. Later, when we were having coffee, he said it was because a director had died suddenly and you had to collect important papers. You never told me about that.'

'Did I not?' his voice rasped. 'I wasn't aware that I had to account to you for everything I did in the line of work.'

'You don't. But I'm surprised you should have forgotten it and thought it was something to do with a customer cancelling a contract.'

'I had forgotten. Unlike you, I don't have the knack of total recall.'

She could tell from the tone of his voice how he must be looking. His lower lip would be jutting out as if he were a petulant child resentful of parental domination. She turned off the tap and began drying the plucked body. Remaining so absorbed in her work that she didn't have to face him she said, 'You haven't told me how well you knew Deirdre.'

'I don't like being interrogated.'

'It's a simple question. If you don't want to answer . . .'

'I'll answer. I hardly knew her.'

Stella reached for a roll of cling-film. 'You knew her well enough to ask her out for a meal.'

'Just what are you getting at?'

At last she looked at him directly. 'Did you have an affair with her?'

He threw back his head and laughed. She recognised it as a false laugh. It was the laugh she heard at office parties when the managing director told a poor joke, or at home when he was making the effort to be sociable to one of her school colleagues.

'What a ridiculous thing to say. An affair? Of course not. Honestly, if it wasn't so absurd, I'd be angry.'

She put the pheasant, now wrapped in cling-film, into the refrigerator.

'What makes you think I might have had an affair?' he went on. 'Come to that, why be mealy-mouthed? Why not say, straight out, "Did you have it off with her?" Or would that be too crude?'

'It is crude.'

'It is. And so am I. You've made that clear enough.'

She went to a formica-topped table where a pot of tea and cup and saucer were standing on a wooden tray. 'I'll have my tea now. You'll stick to whisky?'

'What makes you think I might have had an affair with Deirdre?'

'I didn't think it. I'm asking.'

'That doesn't make sense. Why ask if you haven't thought about it?'

153

She began pouring tea.

'I'm getting a bit fed up with this,' he said. 'You play bloody detective and give the police a lead which could end with your own father under suspicion. You discuss me with him behind my back. And now you accuse me of having an affair. What are you trying to do? Shift the blame for her murder on to me?'

She moved past him.

'Where are you going?' he demanded.

'To drink this in the other room. I don't want to stay in the kitchen all night.'

He followed her into the front room of the cottage which had been furnished with items mostly bought at local auctions. Nothing was new but the room had an air of faded comfort reminiscent of the lounge of a hotel which was once first-class but has long since been down-graded to two stars. Max was already in the room, lying asleep in front of an empty stone grate.

'He must be tired,' she said. 'He didn't pester for tit-bits in the kitchen.'

Between them, by unspoken agreement, whenever there had been a difference and one began talking about the dog, it was a signal to the other that a truce was being offered. Rodney accepted the offer.

'He ran after a rabbit when we were out. I think it must have worn him out.'

'He didn't catch it?'

'Not a chance.'

'Poor old Max.'

'Yes.'

The dog's head lifted. Its sleep had been broken.

'What would you like to do tomorrow?' she asked.

'If it's fine I thought we might go for a swim before breakfast.'

'Not a bad idea. And after?'

'Golf. Healthy relaxation.'

'You play golf, I'll do some gardening. It looks

like . . .' She broke off and stared at the mantelpiece. 'It's gone,' she said. 'That green pot. You know, Sandra Gray made it in the pottery class and gave it to me.'

He followed her gaze. 'You didn't put it away when we left last time?'

'No. Why should I? It's gone.' She stood up. 'I distinctly remember it was there just before we left. There were roses in it, the petals were falling, and I threw them in the dustbin. It was one of the last things I did.'

'It can't have vanished,' he said.

'It has.'

She stooped and felt in the grate. 'Look!' She held up a fragment of fired clay. 'It's been broken.'

'Who the hell broke it?'

'I'm beginning to wonder if . . . There were one or two things in the kitchen. The knife, the serrated one. It was in a slightly different place. The cutlery tray had been shifted. I didn't really think anything of it at the time. I wanted to get on with the pheasant. But I noted it. I mean, it registered on my subconscious.'

'What are you saying?'

'I'm saying I think someone has been in here since we were.'

'A burglar?'

'I don't know. There's nothing much worth stealing, anyway.'

'We'd better look around,' he said, standing up. 'Let's check everywhere and see if anything's missing.'

The cottage had two bedrooms. In the second bedroom she said, 'This chest of drawers has been opened.'

'How do you know?'

'I always square off drawers, but there's one sticking out more than the others. Someone has been looking inside.'

'Quarter of an inch.'

155

'I always square off the drawers.'

He nodded. 'Okay. So we've had an intruder. But why?'

'Why do you think?'

'I don't know. You're the detective, not me.'

She pulled a sour face. 'I think it's connected with Deirdre.'

'For Christ's sake! You'll be saying next that whoever broke in was looking for Deirdre's bracelet.'

'I don't need to. You've just said it for me.'

She spoke calmly, treating his sarcasm as serious comment. For a moment he looked off balance but he recovered with a show of bluster.

'Why search here for the bracelet? That's a ridiculous idea. It's far more likely that someone broke in, knowing this was a holiday cottage, and hoped to find something valuable. I bet if we'd had a hi-fi or a TV set they would have been taken. Even a radio. But thanks to your get-away-from-it-all ideas for a back-to-nature-little-hideaway this place isn't much different from what it was a hundred years ago.'

'You agreed.'

'Sure. And I still do. I don't come here to watch television. But it is isolated. Only Mrs Prentice at the other end of the lane and she's as deaf as a post.'

She straightened the drawer so that it was flush with the other drawers. 'I expect you're right. A casual break-in.'

'We'll ask Mrs Prentice tomorrow if she's seen anyone lurking around.'

He led the way down narrow stairs constructed of solid oak blocks which linked the front living room to the bedroom.

'Can I get you a drink now?' he asked.

'All right. A sherry. And then I'll rustle up something to eat.'

When he returned with the drinks he said, 'There's

no sign of a break-in. All the windows were secured from the inside. Whoever came must have gone in through the front door. That means a key – two keys – were used.'

'A professional job?'

'The police could do it.'

'But why?'

'Your friend Cook. Or a cop in this area. Under cover. Off the record. You said yourself you didn't think Cook believed you when you said you'd found the imp by the roadside. He may think we're hiding the bracelet and got someone to search this place before we arrived. For all we know a search was made only hours ago.'

'But the broken pot?'

'Tipped up to see if it held anything and it slipped from the grasp.'

'I hate all this,' she said with sudden fierceness. 'It spoils things. Makes everything' – she glanced round the room – 'soiled.'

'I hate it as much as you. More. I could be in the firing line. I helped your father to steal a bracelet. An accessory after the fact. Concealing vital evidence.'

She looked troubled. 'You don't think . . . I mean, it couldn't have been Dad . . .'

'What? Broke in here?'

'No.' She lowered her voice to a whisper. 'Killed Deirdre.'

He shook his head. 'Not him. He was stupid to have an affair with someone like her, but no, not him.'

'He told you he was sitting in the car and then he heard a scream. He didn't do anything for a minute or two and when he did turn the car and drive back he saw her body. That's what he told you?'

'Didn't he tell you the same thing today at lunch?'

'We didn't actually talk about that part. I'd only gone to warn him about the imp, after all.'

'You know something,' he said, toying with a whisky

157

glass, twisting it so that light fell on cut crystal, 'if I could live that day again I'd never have lent him the car, and certainly not gone to the wood with him. But I owed him a favour, and it seemed like a good way of repaying it. Normal obligation. I need my head tested. Only fools believe in moral obligations.'

FOUR

On a morning with darting glittering specks on a sunlit sea they ran across sand-dunes, jumping clear of tufts of marram grass, and raced down the beach.

He hit the water first and cried out, 'God, it's cold,' before plunging. She waded after him, her body tensing against the chill which clawed up legs and thighs. 'Come on, Max,' she called. 'It's lovely.' But Max was more intent on investigating and marking a clump of grass.

After ten minutes they'd had enough and made their way up the beach to where they'd dropped towels. As they dried themselves he looked at her approvingly and said, 'You'd look really good in a bikini.'

'So you've said before. Thanks for the compliment but I prefer what I'm wearing.'

'Too bad.'

'Now take those thoughts out of your mind and concentrate on what you'd like for breakfast. There's a choice. Kippers or eggs and bacon.'

He draped the towel round his shoulders and began walking towards the spot where they'd parked the car. 'Come on, Max,' he said. 'Dogs like us must only think of brekkie-breks. Anything else is naughty.' To her he called out, 'Kippers should meet the need of the inner dog.'

'I need to go to the shops.'

'Okay. You take the car. I'll walk to the golf course.'

'The exercise will do you good.'

'That's right.'

'Any idea when you'll be back?'

'Before midday.'

'See you then.'

'If not before. I'm only going to do nine holes.'

'Are you sure you don't want to wait till I've done the shopping?'

'Quite sure. I'll walk it. Get healthily tired. Darling.'

She drove to the nearest town, a place so unremarkable with its Victorian and Edwardian villas and cottages that it could only be described in guide books as a typical East Anglian town. It had no important historical associations and seemed to exist simply to accommodate and provide for people fortunate enough to be satisfied with ordinary lives; it was a haven of unstriving anonymity and passive surviving.

After calling at the newsagent and the butcher she went to a chemist's shop to buy sun-tan lotion. It was only when she returned to the car-park with her purchases that what had been a routine outing became something different. As she unlocked the door she saw a note taped to the steering wheel. Reaching inside she tore it off. In capitals the note said: ASK YOUR HUSBAND WHO GAVE DEIRDRE THE SCORPION.

She swung round as if expecting to find someone right behind her, and then her gaze raced round the car-park searching for the unknown messenger who had not only left the note but managed to open the car door. She saw a woman unloading provisions from a trolley into a car. Stella ran across.

'Excuse me, but you didn't by any chance notice anyone near my car – that one over there?'

The woman shook her head. 'No. Why? Has it been vandalised?'

'I think someone tried to break into it, but I don't

160

think anything's been taken.' She moved away.

'I didn't see anyone.'

'All right. Thanks.' Stella hurried to the car.

For a few moments she sat in the driver's seat collecting her thoughts. Whoever had the skill to open the car door must have been the person who had the skill to enter and search the cottage As for the note, it must refer to the scorpion on the bracelet. The implication was obvious. Rodney had given Deirdre the scorpion charm.

Although she was staring ahead at a brick building with corrugated iron roof her vision was the memory of a man with a long face, scraggy neck and starched white collar saying, 'You will tell me if you have any ideas, won't you. *We must co-operate on this.*'

She had sensed then that Jameson suspected Rodney. Had he or a hired agent been following her since their meeting? Was the note intended to push her into extricating a confession from Rodney by persistent questioning?

Knuckles rapping at the window beside her caused her to jump in her seat. She turned. Outside, an unduly handsome young man, blue eyes twinkling, white teeth flashing, was holding up a paper bag. It contained her sun-tan lotion. 'Yours?' he enquired.

She unwound the window.

'Thanks. I must have dropped it as I got in.'

She took the bag.

'I couldn't help seeing what it was,' he said, 'and if I may say so, lilies need no gilding.' His smile was more than a sign of goodwill; it was predatory.

She wound up the window fast and switched on the ignition. Then she backed out so quickly she almost crashed into another car. It was with pleasure that she noticed the smile had gone from the stranger's face. He was gaping at her sudden manoeuvre. The car blazed out of the car-park.

161

She drove fast and, two miles out of town, turned off the road and bumped down the rutted track bouncing the car as if it were a rubber ball. Straight into the garage without the usual check that she was correctly aligned. She switched off and slumped. Thank God to be back, she thought. She wanted to get indoors to collect her thoughts before Rodney arrived.

A noise behind made her turn. The garage had suddenly become dark. A clang as the metal door shut. She flung open the car door and dashed to the door of the garage. It was shut tight. Banging her fists on it she shouted, 'Let me out,' but even as she struck she knew it was a useless effort. Whoever had closed the door intended to trap her.

Daylight entered through a barred window but it would be impossible to escape even if she smashed the glass. Who had shut her in and why? Seized by momentary panic she screamed, 'Let me out!'

The door was a sliding up-and-over type and couldn't have closed without someone pulling it down. It locked automatically and this prevented anyone inside the garage from prising it up.

Her panic subsided. Max had been left alone, shut in the cottage; Rodney was playing golf; Mrs Prentice at the other end of the lane was deaf. It was unlikely that anyone would hear her cries although sometimes walkers and hikers came this way. She opened the car door and pressed the horn. Three short blasts: three long: three short: the SOS was repeated a dozen times. Then, afraid of running down the battery she climbed in and sat down.

The note, tucked in a pocket by the dashboard, caught her attention. She picked it up and read again. ASK YOUR HUSBAND WHO GAVE DEIRDRE THE SCORPION. Supposing she did ask him, and supposing he replied, 'I gave it to her', what would come next? She would ask why.

162

All the charms seemed to have some significance for the giver. What was the link between a scorpion and Rodney? He had been born under the astrological sign of Scorpio on November the thirteenth. Was the token to remind Deirdre of his birthday?

And then she remembered a date which had appeared more than once in the Press cuttings. Deirdre Jameson had been born on October the thirty-first. Hallowe'en. One journalist had pointed out that her birthday was on the last day of the old Celtic year, its night being the time when witches and warlocks went abroad to work their mischief. The date fell within the House of Scorpio. So Rodney and Deirdre shared the same astrological sign. And there was a numerical connection, thirteen being the reverse of thirty-one. A tiny scorpion for her bracelet would make an ideal reminder of their association.

She put down the note and pressed the horn again. With thirteen on her mind she sent out thirteen SOS signals. A total silence followed. The rasping horn had even quietened the faintly audible birdsong. She could imagine Max, lying on the hearth rug, raising his sleepy head before subsiding again into slumber. Rodney might be about halfway through his round of golf – if he was playing golf.

A flash of intuition illuminated a corner of her mind she'd deliberately kept dark. Although it would have been impossible for Rodney to have left the note he could easily have closed the garage door on her. She had last seen him walking jauntily away, bag of clubs slung over one shoulder, soon disappearing from sight behind gorse bushes. At the time she had thought it rather strange he shouldn't have waited for her to return from shopping and then use the car to drive himself to the golf course. She had said, half in jest, 'The walk will do you good,' and he had unsmilingly replied, 'That's right.' And his last word to her had been 'Darling', spoken as sarcasm, not an endearment.

He could have concealed himself behind bushes until she returned and then crept out to slam the garage door. But why should he want to trap her, unless . . . the thought was too terrible to contemplate . . . unless he wanted her out of the way for good, unless he wanted her dead. She could shout and bang the car horn until the battery died and no-one would hear her . . . I won't think of such things, she told herself. She pressed the horn again. One long blast.

No response.

She climbed out of the car and went to the window. She pulled each bar in turn but all were firmly embedded in brickwork. Glancing up she saw that wooden rafters met at the apex of the roof. A felt lining lay beneath the tiles. There was no way out through the roof.

The view through the rain-stained window was of a thick clump of broom, its blossoms a brilliant yellow, and behind, the darker outline of trees in a wood. It was a scene which had previously gladdened her; the unspoiled backdrop to a secluded country cottage, somewhere remote from suburbia and commuter-land, a place where one could think about communing with nature and even Mother Nature herself.

But Mother Nature was no mother in human terms; she was impersonal, intimidatingly indifferent. Stella turned away from the window with a feeling akin to dull, despondent fear.

An hour passed. Rodney should be back by now. She pressed the horn again and waited. More SOS signals. How long would the battery last? She got out of the car and for the next half hour struggled to lever up the door with the aid of spanners, the car-jack and a screwdriver. Her efforts failed.

Wearily she returned to the car to sit down. At least I've got some food, she thought. Raw meat. And there was water in the car's tank. She could last for days.

I'll give it another quarter of an hour, she thought, and then I'll find a way to jam the car horn and while it's blaring away I'll bash the door with a spanner and make a frightful din. Rodney must be home and he's sure to hear.

Unless . . .

Why should he want me to starve to death? Keep me here until I'm dead? So that he could bury me and no-one discover the grave?

Their married life. Hadn't it been happy enough? Admittedly he had been more keen on the intimate side than she, but otherwise they got along well enough. And if sometimes she had suspected that a night away had been spent in what he would have called 'a one-night stand' she had not asked embarrassing questions and, indeed, had blotted thoughts of infidelity from her mind.

And then she remembered that three, or perhaps four years ago he hadn't come home on the night of his birthday. It was the one night of the year when she tried to be the perfect, pliant partner in bed, but he hadn't come home. He had phoned to say he was being kept late at a meeting and had to stay overnight. Had he been with Deirdre?

This is ridiculous, she thought. I must get a grip on myself. She pressed the horn. It sounded weaker. Perhaps it would be unwise to jam it.

She got out of the car, picked up the heaviest spanner and went to the door. Crash, crash, crash. She beat the door as if hammering out all the fears and frustrations of a lifetime.

No result, except for dented metal.

Back to the window. The position of the sun had changed and the broom's blossoms were in shadow and the outline of the trees menacingly dark. She went to a switch which should have lighted the garage with a neon strip but when she flicked it the strip remained pallidly lifeless. Either the filament or the fuse had blown.

A new surge of panic was smothered by repeating over and over again to herself – I shall be all right, I shall be all right, I shall be all right.

But she wasn't sure she would be all right.

The hours crawled by. Periodically she sounded the horn or banged the door and shouted. And then she had what seemed a clever idea. She would start the car, drive it forward a yard or so up to the wall, put it into reverse gear and tread hard on the accelerator. By using the car as a battering ram she might burst open the door.

She fastened her safety belt and started the engine. Forward, change gear and, stabbing down her foot, back. The rear of the car crashed against the door. The impact jarred Stella's body but didn't shift the door. She drove forward and repeated the process with the same result.

Exhaust fumes were filling the garage. Realising the danger of carbon monoxide poisoning she switched off the engine. The stink of exhaust made her feel slightly dizzy. Taking care not to breathe deeply she got out of the car and, holding her breath, hurried to the window. Within seconds most of the glass had been knocked out by a spanner and the fumes began drifting out. Within minutes the air was pure and fresh. But the noise hadn't brought anyone to her rescue and the declining sun was throwing long shadows from the bushes.

A feeling of hopelessness swept over her and tears came to her eyes. Unless Rodney had suffered some accident while playing golf (in which case someone would have called to tell her) he must be back at the cottage and have heard the violent crashing of car against metal door. His refusal to come to her aid could only mean he was responsible for locking her in. What

166

was his motive? Was he punishing her for telling her father that she knew about the bracelet? If so, how long would the punishment last? Or, more sinister, was he afraid she was getting too close to the discovery that he had murdered Deirdre? The suppressed fear that he wanted her out of the way could no longer be suppressed.

She blew her nose and dried her eyes. Fury at her predicament welled up and ignited a burning hatred for her husband.

She pressed her face against the window bars and screamed, 'You won't get away with this, you rotten bastard!'

FIVE

When he left the course, his wallet thicker by the addition of a five pound note, Rodney was well satisfied with himself. His drives had been straight, his swing just about right, and his putting more accurate than usual. A good round of golf always put him in a good mood and today was no exception. But he wished he'd been more agreeable to Stella before leaving and resolved to make it up to her when he got back.

On reaching the cottage he was surprised to find the back door still locked. The garage was closed which meant Stella must be home. Perhaps for some reason she'd entered by the front door and not bothered to unlock the back. He used his keys and as he stepped into the kitchen he called out a cheerful, 'I'm home.'

A voice behind said quietly, 'And about time. I've got you covered. Any aggro and you'll be paralysed from the waist down.'

Something hard jabbed his spine. 'I know the exact spot,' the voice continued, 'and we don't want to lose our manhood, do we? Now get on in.'

He heard the door slammed behind him.

'Keep walking.'

As they entered the front room Max came forward wagging his tail.

'Good boy,' said the voice.

Max's tail swished even quicker.

'Okay, Mr Best. Sit down.'

Rodney went to his customary chair, ratten-backed and foam-cushioned.

The intruder wore a black hood over his head; there were gaps for his eyes and mouth. Tall and broad-chested, he wore a lightweight grey suit; his left fist gripped a short-barrelled black automatic pistol.

'Right,' he said. 'Now you can answer a few questions and I want the right answers. No messing.'

His accent was London East End overlaid with traces of American as if he'd spent his formative years watching imported B movies.

'Who are you?'

'That doesn't matter. We're not going to socialise.'

Max had gone back to the hearth rug and flopped down. The man tilted his head in the dog's direction. 'He's got sense. You'd better have.'

Rodney sized up distances. It would be impossible to spring at the man without getting shot and the telephone was out of reach.

'You needn't think about that, Mr Best. The line's cut.'

'Where's my wife?'

'I thought you'd never ask,' came the reply in a voice which was a fair imitation of a well-known camp comedian.

'You haven't . . .'

'Haven't what, Mr Best? Roddy.' The name was spoken tauntingly. It flashed through Rodney's mind that he was facing a psychopath or a sadist.

'Where is she?'

'Now I do like a bit of husbandly concern. That does you credit, Roddy. Considering your past history, I'm really impressed.'

'What do you want?'

'Does wifey know about your past history? Playing the field? I won't use crude words. She wouldn't like that.'

169

As Rodney wondered how the man had learned of Stella's distaste for coarse language he heard the sound of a distant car horn.

'Hark, hark, the bloody lark,' said the man.

The horn peeped out SOS in morse code.

'Lucky it's only us likely to hear that, Roddy. Otherwise I might have to do something nasty. Like giving the lady wife a tranquilliser.'

'You've locked her in the garage.'

'Jesus, you're smart. That dog isn't the only bright one round here.'

'Why don't you tell me what you want?'

'What do you think I want, Roddy?'

'I've no idea.'

The black hood moved as the man shook his head. 'You aren't so bright. Think. Just think why someone like me would be in a dump like this talking to someone like you.'

'I don't know.'

'Then I'll clue you. You like to play home and away. But you get more away wins than you get at home.'

An uneasy awareness that the man knew about his private life added a different sort of fear to the fear Rodney already felt.

'I don't know what you're talking about,' he said.

'Women, Roddy. Women. One woman in particular. You know who I mean.'

Deirdre. The man had come about Deirdre. Did he want the bracelet?

'I don't know who you mean.'

'Oh yes, you do. Scorpion. I won't say more.'

'Deirdre?'

'Yes, Roddy, Deirdre. Wickedly cut down in the prime of life. And by you.'

'This is absurd. I didn't kill her. I never saw her that day.'

The man gave a quiet laugh. 'Don't wriggle, Roddy.'

'I'm not wriggling.'

'You're wriggling all right. Shit-scared and wriggling. That's you. But it won't do you no good. I'm not leaving till I get a signed confession out of you.'

'I didn't kill her.'

'Ha bloody ha.'

'I swear I didn't kill her.'

'No? Then who did?'

'Are you working for William Jameson?'

'I ask the questions. If you didn't do her, who did?'

'I don't know.'

'You don't think it was your wife's randy old Dad. That's what you told her. But maybe you were being clever. I know she don't think it was him.'

Rodney was taken aback. 'You're in no position to say what either of us think.'

'Correction. I am in a very good position. None better except the pillow itself.'

It took two seconds for the significance of this statement to sink in. 'Is this place bugged?'

'You're smart. Amazing deduction. I reckon you might even have the edge on your dog.'

'You broke into this place, searched it, and planted bugs.'

'If one of my hands wasn't occupied I'd give you a round of applause.'

It was disconcerting to hear ironic comment coming from an expressionless hood but even more unsettling to wonder how many private conversations had been overheard and possibly recorded on tape.

Sensing the thoughts chasing through his captive's mind the man asked, 'Worried about what I heard? I'll tell you. I heard the lot. Everything. And incidentally, Roddy, when a lady says she's tired and got a bit of a headache it isn't nice manners to say, "That's about par for the course." It's not sensitive.'

Rodney gazed at a point past the man's left shoulder

with an unfocused blankness in his eyes. It was an expression practised in his early days as a salesman and used whenever he was obliged to listen to a customer's long-winded complaint. It was a look of total impassivity.

'What you should say is, "Can I get you an aspirin, my darling."'

Rodney gave no sign of having heard the taunting advice.

In a harsher voice the man asked, 'Was killing Deirdre better than killing that poor bloody chicken?'

No reply.

'You strangled her like she was a chicken. Right?'

No reply.

'I hope you're not going to force me to use strong arm stuff, Roddy. I can be a right mean bastard if I have to.'

The man took a pace forward and raised his gun hand. 'Do you want this across your chops? Broken teeth would spoil your beauty.'

'I did not strangle Deirdre Jameson.'

The man lowered his hand. 'That's better. You weren't straight with wifey, were you? First, you make out you couldn't remember what happened to you when Deirdre met father-in-law. Was it you were called away because someone had died in Leeds or was it a customer screaming about a contract? You messed that up, Roddy. Of course you couldn't tell her the truth which was neither. You fixed it so you'd be called away to the phone. There was no director in Leeds, no customer, nothing, nil, zero, zilch. Just you giving the poor old sod the chance for a bit of the other with a bird you wanted to drop. Trouble was you didn't know your own mind and when you tried to start up with her again she didn't want to know. She told you to get lost. You were rejected. It began to burn you up. In the end you decided if you couldn't have her, no-one else would.'

'That's rubbish, and you know it's rubbish.'

172

The hooded head shook slowly from side to side.

'How could I have killed her? I was nowhere near the place.'

The head continued to shake. 'Wrong again, Roddy. Don't lie.'

Already afraid, the cold certainty in the man's voice sent a shiver of apprehension through Rodney. His hands gripped the sides of the chair as if they were handrails on a rolling ship.

He heard the car-horn again. A prolonged blast followed by SOS.

'If that stupid bitch doesn't belt up,' said the man, 'I'll go and do her.'

To Rodney's immense relief the honking stopped.

'Now then, Roddy. I want this over with. I haven't got all day. You going to sign a confession or am I going to have to get rough with you?'

'I'm not confessing to something I didn't do.'

'You did it, and what's more you know I know you did it.'

'No.'

'Because you weren't there, you say?'

'That's right.'

'Where were you?'

'At company headquarters. Romford.'

'Bloody liar. When you let your father-in-law have your car for the day you sent someone else to deliver it. Right?'

'Right.'

'You were tied up at the time?'

'Yes.'

'Not true. A meeting had been cancelled. You could have delivered the car yourself. But instead, you sent a mate. A junior. And what did you do? I'll tell you. You got hold of another of the firm's cars and followed the old goat.'

Although he was seated and gripping the chair's

173

sides, Rodney felt giddy. He closed his eyes. His eyes remained tightly shut as the man continued, 'You tailed father-in-law all the way to the place he met Deirdre. And you followed them to the wood. And you watched from the wood. And when Deirdre ran from the car you jumped. You dragged her into the wood and threatened to kill her unless she came back to you. She refused. You lost your cool and killed her.'

Rodney opened his eyes. The giddiness had passed but his mouth was so dry that when he tried to speak the words wouldn't come. He swallowed and with an effort said, 'That's partly true. I did follow. I parked not far from the place where they were due to meet but when she didn't turn up after an hour I decided she wasn't coming and I left. I drove back to Romford. I never went near the wood.'

'Christ! Don't treat me like a moron! You went there, and you killed her.' The man advanced and raised his arm threateningly. 'You say once more you didn't do it and I'll duff you good and proper.'

Rodney shrunk back in the chair.

'Come on,' the man shouted. 'Admit!'

'No.'

'I won't only do you over, I'll do that bitch over too. How'd you like that?'

Rodney tensed his muscles, bracing himself to spring.

'She's a good-looker, your wife. It would be a real pleasure to screw her.'

Rodney sprang, but it was a slow and clumsy movement. The man side-stepped and brought down his gun on the side of Rodney's head. He blacked out.

When he came to he was securely tied to the chair with a length of washing line the man must have fetched from the garden. His ankles seemed riveted to the legs of the chair and his wrists clamped to its arms. A length of line had been tightly wound round his body and knotted on his chest. His head ached painfully.

'You awake at last, Roddy? I was beginning to worry. You can't take it, can you? You don't have to. Say you'll write out a confession and I'll undo your hands. When you've signed I'll leave and you can finish untying yourself. Then you can free wifey from the lock-up. I won't trouble you no more.'

'I didn't do it.'

'You followed the old man.'

'Yes. But not to the wood. I never went there.'

'Sorry, Roddy. I'm going to have to refresh your memory. Try a little gentle persuasion.'

A crack echoed through the cottage as the man's hand struck the side of Rodney's face.

SIX

Stella leaned against the car staring at the barred window space as if willing the bars to part like the waters of the Red Sea. If a way could be found to force the two centre bars apart, to bend them into bow shape, she might be able to squeeze through the gap.

She went to the tool-box and examined its contents. Nothing there which could be used to prise apart the bars. And then she noticed the jack used for lifting the car when a wheel change was needed. It was an ordinary screw jack operated by a handle which turned interconnecting cogs. Thoughtfully she picked it up and took it to the window where she placed it on its side. It fitted exactly between the bars. The problem was how to exert sufficient pressure to rotate the cogs.

The car was powerful enough to turn the handle if she could harness it. It would be a slow process, forward to the end of the garage would just about move one cog. The harness would have to be disconnected, the car backed, the harness fitted again, and then another cog turned. What could she use as a harness?

This problem was solved when she remembered a length of reinforced nylon rope which had once been used to tow her car and was now lying coiled up in an old cupboard at the side of the garage together with a can of multi-purpose oil, rags, and car cleaning materials.

She wound the rope round the spar between front and rear doors and led it to the handle. By twisting the handle she achieved maximum tension. She was now ready to drive the car forward.

If it works, she thought, I ought to get the Heath Robinson award for inventiveness. Here goes.

The car edged forward until its fender touched the wall. She quickly switched off the engine and jumped out. 'Success,' she said aloud and her eyes were alight with delight at mind's conquest over matter. For a few moments she almost forgot her predicament. The cogs had moved and part of the cement footing had crumbled. One bar was slightly distorted near the base.

She took all the spanners from the tool-box and by laying them on the ledge, their jaws clamping the bars, she built a small foundation for the jack.

The next drive was even more successful. A bulge had developed in what was the weaker of the two bars. She went through the laborious task of dismantling the harness, backing the car, and refastening it. Her fear that the car's spar might not be strong enough to take the strain hadn't been justified; it was the bar and not the spar which was yielding.

On the fourth twist of the jack-handle the bar snapped like a dry stick.

She examined the damage. Gripping the lower part of the bar with her hands and working it back and forth like a lever it gradually came free of the cement base which had already crumbled. At last there seemed space enough to crawl through if she cared to risk being stuck halfway.

Once, as a child, she had seen her father struggle to turn a car tyre inside out so as to make an ornamental urn which, when painted white and filled with soil, would serve to hold a small bush. 'I won't be beaten,' he had said repeatedly, sweat pouring down his forehead. She said it now. I won't be beaten.

Using the car as a springboard she hoist herself up and into the space between the bars. It was a painful effort but she managed to work herself through and fall clear on the far side.

Picking herself up, she brushed soil from her clothes and then, jaw firmly set, hurried towards the cottage. Unless Rodney had excellent reasons for ignoring her distress signals she would inform him she wanted a divorce. Her father would act on her behalf and all future communications should be addressed to him.

Max greeted her at the back door. She gave him a brief pat and said, 'Where's your master? I want a word with him.' As if understanding her the dog turned and went towards the front room. At the doorway it paused, looked back, and then walked on. She followed.

Controlled anger was replaced by horror when she saw the man she intended to divorce bound hand and foot to a chair, a gag in his mouth, and his face grazed and bruised.

After removing the gag her agitated fingers began untying knots. 'What happened? Who did it?'

'You're all right?' he asked.

'Fine.'

'Thank God.'

'Who tied you up?'

'I don't know. He wore a hood. A big guy. Tried to make me confess to murdering Deirdre.'

'But you didn't. You didn't confess.'

'No way. But he knew a hell of a lot about me. And us. This place was bugged.'

The washing line began to slacken and he moved his arms.

'How do you feel?' she asked. 'You look a mess.'

'He wasn't gentle, but no bones broken. I think. My head's sore where he thumped me. I was out cold for a bit.'

His arms were free. She knelt on the carpet and began untying the knots by his ankles. 'Do you need a doctor?'

'No. I'm all right.'

178

'What about the police?'

'I'd thought about that,' he said, 'but I'm not sure. Not tell them yet, I think.' As he kicked an ankle free he added, 'We'll talk it over.'

'Where is he now? This man?'

'He heard all the noise you were making. Went to the window to look out and saw a couple of ramblers walking across the common. He said if the noise brought them over they'd be sorry. I think he was bluffing. Anyway I told him there were plenty of ramblers this time of year and sometimes they called in here for a drink of water. I think that did the trick. He suddenly said, "You can sweat this out. I'm pushing. Hard cheese if you and her get stuck here for good." Then he left.'

'Left? Just like that?'

He managed to stand while she, crouching, undid the last knots.

'Yes, just like that. I think he recognised the law of diminishing returns. The more he knocked me about the less capable I'd be of doing anything except pass out. And he might just have believed I was telling the truth, and I didn't murder Deirdre.'

Now completely free he stretched and flexed arm and leg muscles. She stood up. 'I don't want to stay here,' she said.

'Go home?'

'Yes. It's been completely spoiled.' She gave him a searching look. 'Do you feel up to the journey?'

He gave a slight smile. 'Tea laced with brandy should set me up.' His hand caressed the bump on his head. 'Tender.'

'I'll make the tea; then we'll pack and go.' Very gently she reached out and touched an unmarked part of his face. It was a loving gesture. 'You stay here. I'll bring it in.'

While he drank tea heavily fortified by brandy she

179

told him of how she had escaped from the garage. And then, without altering the tone of her voice she said, 'Did you give Deirdre a scorpion for her bracelet?'

'Yes. How did you know?'

She told him about the note left on the steering wheel.

Choosing his words as though he was stepping through a minefield he told her how he had first met Deirdre by chance at a roadside café. At the time of the TV commercial the affair had been going for nearly a year but he was finding it a strain. 'I know it sounds melodramatic,' he said, 'but I reckon that if she'd been living in mediaeval times she'd have been burned as a witch. She had the power to fascinate.'

Gazing out of the window at the common Stella asked, 'Did you give her the witch for her bracelet?'

'No. That was someone else.'

'Go on.'

'Even after we'd parted she sometimes rang me at the office. She didn't want me, but she didn't want me to be able to do without her. I knew Ambrose was seeing her from time to time. She made sure I knew. Tried to make me jealous. And, to be honest, in a funny way I was a bit. When I lent him my car I borrowed another and followed him. It was crazy. I don't know what I expected to gain. He waited at a pub for Deirdre but when she didn't turn up, I left.'

'Didn't he see you?'

'I parked some way off and watched through a hedge.'

'And then?'

'I went back to Romford. I was wondering when I'd see him, and, if he didn't turn up, how I'd get home. But he arrived. Distraught. He told me that Deirdre had been murdered and he'd moved her body into some bushes but not taken the bracelet. And the bracelet would be a clue to a connection between him and her.'

Still avoiding meeting his eyes she said, 'So you went back with him to get the bracelet, and that's why you arrived home late with a story about having been kept at a meeting and losing your wallet when a couple of thugs bumped into you.'

'I'm sorry.'

'I'm sorry too. Perhaps if I'd been more . . . Oh, let's not go into that.'

'No. Let's not.'

'The point is,' she said, looking at him directly, 'that you didn't kill Deirdre although you were still involved with her.'

'Not really involved.'

'Involved or not. It doesn't matter. What matters is that you didn't kill her.' She reached out and held his hand. 'That's all that matters. Honestly.'

A slight noise by the door. 'What was that?' she asked.

The door swung open. 'It's only me,' said a voice.

The hooded man was covering them with his gun.

'Pity about that,' he said. 'I was hoping to hear something interesting. But you, Roddy, are keeping up the act with her.' He turned his head towards Stella. 'If you believe what he tells you, you'd believe anything. He's in it up to his neck. Or should I say – up to Deirdre Jameson's neck.'

Rodney began to stand up but was waved down by a gun hand.

'Sit still, Roddy. I shouldn't have left you to sweat. That was a mistake.' He waved his gun in Stella's direction. 'You can pick up that rope, sweetheart, and tie him up again. Come on. On your feet, darling.'

She stood up. The washing line was on the carpet close to where the man was standing.

'If you don't co-operate,' he said, 'you'll be a widow. I can arrange that very easily.' He pointed the gun at Rodney.

181

She didn't move. 'Hurry up, sweetheart. Or do you want him out of the way? Do you want to be a widow?'

She moved forward hesitantly. With his free hand the man grabbed her arm and yanked her towards him. 'Get cracking, darling.'

Several things happened at once. Stella screamed. Max, dormant until then, forgot age and infirmities and sprang like a young terrier at the man's legs and fastened his teeth into the right calf. The man fired at Max. Rodney hurled himself from the chair and with a body charge sent the man reeling so that he tripped over the rug and fell. Max gave a terrible howl and blood began pouring from a wound in one of his hind legs. The man, his head having hit the edge of the stone hearth, lay still.

Stella knelt beside Max and Rodney went to the man.

'Oh, Max!'

'Christ, he's unconscious.'

'Max!' She turned to Rodney who was holding the man's wrist.

'I think he's had it,' he said. 'No pulse beat.'

'Are you sure?'

'Fairly sure.'

'We must get an ambulance. Call the police.'

'The phone's been cut.'

She was cradling Max who whimpered softly. 'I've got to get Max to the vet. I'll call the police from his surgery. You wait here in case he recovers.' She stood up. 'You'll have to help me carry him to the car.'

'Just a sec.' He had been unfastening the hood and now he pulled it off. 'I thought so. It's the guy who's been following me.' Very gently he pulled back an eyelid and placed the ball of his finger on the eyeball. There was no reaction. 'He's dead,' said Rodney.

'Come on. Help me. Max is bleeding badly. There's a first-aid kit in the car. We'll bandage the leg.'

'I'll carry him. You take my keys and open the garage.

I'll come with you now. No point in staying here.'

It was she who nursed Max on her bloodstained dress while Rodney drove.

First Deirdre, and now this, he thought. It wouldn't be possible to protect Ambrose any longer. The truth would have to be told and Ambrose would have to explain why he allowed Deirdre to run from his car and didn't follow, or respond at once when he heard her scream. And he might be believed, and he might not.

His train of thought was interrupted by the sound of Stella sobbing quietly. He glanced sideways and to his relief saw that Max, panting rapidly, seemed to be all right. At least he was still alive. But tears were running down Stella's cheeks.

'We'll soon be there,' he said, 'Max will pull through.'

'He saved me,' she sobbed.

SEVEN

An unmarked police car drove up a gravel drive which led to a Georgian house on the outskirts of Ipswich. When it stopped two men in plain clothes got out and walked purposefully to the front door.

It was some time before their bell-ring was answered and then the door was opened by a pale-faced woman who wore a long grey dress and, even though it was summer and a warm day, she was pulling a black shawl across her shoulders. Both men immediately noticed circles of badly applied rouge on her pallid cheeks and that the red gash of lipstick on her thin lips was smeared at one corner.

The first man showed his card. 'Detective Inspector Cook,' he said. 'I'd like to speak to Mr Jameson.'

'I know. You've been here before.'

Cook nodded. 'You're Miss Jameson if I remember rightly.'

'You do. You'd better come in . . . William! It's the police.'

She showed them into the drawing room which Stella had found peculiarly lifeless with its stale sealed-in atmosphere and faded furnishings. As she did so she surreptitiously fastened the top button of her dress.

Jameson entered rubbing his eyes. 'Thought I heard the door-bell. I was having a cat-nap out at the back.'

'Sorry to have disturbed you, sir . . . Just a moment, Miss Jameson. I'd prefer you to stay, if you don't mind.'

Stopped trying to slip out of the room unnoticed she went reluctantly to a chair, picked up some knitting and began to knit. Her face was expressionless as the marble of the fireplace.

'Please sit down,' said Jameson. 'Have you got news for me? I must say it's about time.'

'This is Detective Sergeant Pinkney,' said Cook. 'He's been working with me on the case.'

'Yes. Quite,' Jameson replied, scarcely glancing at the funereal-faced Pinkney. 'Now then. What news?'

Cook settled himself in a chair which creaked uneasily under his weight. 'I assume you know the fate that's befallen your Mr Roberts?'

'Roberts? No. What's that?'

'An unfortunate accident while he was trying to intimidate someone he suspected of murdering your lady friend.'

'That fellow Best?'

'Precisely.'

William Jameson frowned. 'I trust he wasn't doing anything unethical. I can't condone that. What sort of accident? Is he in hospital?'

'No, the mortuary.'

'What!'

'Dead. I don't wish to sound heartless, Mr Jameson, but you knew from the start what my views were when you engaged a private detective. As a rule they do nothing but interfere and muddy the waters.'

Miss Jameson crouched over her knitting and needles clicked with a steady rhythm like a metronome on allegro. She was working on the sleeve of a Fair Isle sweater and seemed to have cut herself off from the others.

'Dead,' Jameson echoed. 'How did it happen?'

'According to statements made by Mr and Mrs Best,' Cook began, and he related the events which had taken place at the cottage.

185

'And is that all you've come for?' asked Jameson when the account was finished. 'Rather a waste of police time and ratepayers' money to send two men to tell me about Mr Roberts. I'm not responsible for him, you know. Whatever he did was of his own initiative.'

'I wouldn't be too sure of that, sir. But we won't go into the law concerning principal and agent. There is something else.'

'And what might that be?'

'Mr Best was very co-operative. We now have a much better picture of circumstances surrounding your lady friend's death. It's clear that on the fatal Thursday she drove from here to a pub some miles away called the Cock Inn. Here she met a gentleman and went off with him in a car – not his own car but a car he'd borrowed for the day. Together they drove to the lane by Santer's Wood. According to a statement we have from the gentleman in question there was a quarrel. The lady said she didn't wish to see him any more. He argued the point. In the end she jumped out of the car and ran away.'

Jameson leaned forward, his neck pressed against a stiff white collar on which a speck of blood showed he'd cut himself while shaving that morning. His weathered hands gripped the sides of his wing-chair.

'And this so-called gentleman ran after her?'

'Not according to his statement.'

'He's not admitting anything. Is that it?' The words shot spitting-fast out of Jameson's mouth.

'Not quite, sir.' Cook spoke in the measured tones of someone who will not be hurried but intends to set the pace of any conversation. 'He admits he eventually went after her but it was too late. She was dead. He panicked. He realised he was in a vulnerable position and he is a highly-placed professional man. His priority was to avoid any scandal. After pulling her body out of sight he hurried back to London. To Romford, to be exact.'

'The bracelet. He took the bracelet?'

'Not then. That's another story. We mustn't digress.'

'Digress from what?' James spluttered. 'It seems you fellows are easily taken in by stories told by "highly-placed professional men".'

'Not at all, sir. But one thing at a time. You must bear with me.'

Jameson sat back. 'Very well. Take your time. But I warn you, I am far from satisfied with what you've told me and if you can't improve on it I shall complain to your superior, Mr Vesty – not that he has been much help so far – no, on second thoughts I shall complain to the Chief Constable.'

'I hope that will not be necessary, sir,' said Cook evenly. 'Assuming that this gentleman's statement is substantially correct and he panicked and drove back to Romford – and there are witnesses to corroborate his time of arrival – it was roughly the same time that the lady's car was noticed parked in a side street in Ipswich. Now, he couldn't possibly have returned to Romford and simultaneously driven a car from the Cock Inn to Ipswich.'

In the silence which followed the sound of clicking needles seemed amplified.

At last Jameson spoke. The fire had gone from his voice. 'Someone must have driven it. But who?'

'That is the vital question. Who? We fingerprinted the car, as you know. There were no prints we couldn't account for. Not that this surprised us. It was a purely routine exercise. At that time we thought the lady had met someone and been given a lift from Ipswich or had hitch-hiked her way to the neighbourhood of Santer's Wood.'

'I'm baffled. I don't know what to say. Where do we go from there?'

Detective Sergeant Pinkney who had been gazing lugubriously at a dark still life of fruit and flowers which

187

hung behind Jameson's left shoulder switched his attention to Cook and for a moment his face lost its funereal solemnity. Like Jameson, he was interested to learn what line Cook was going to take. Only the woman seated on the far side of the room seemed unconcerned with events.

'We now move into the field of speculation,' said Cook, 'but first one more question. It is important. When the lady left on that Thursday did you see her off? Did you go with her to the car to say goodbye?'

Jameson thought. 'No. The rep from Forsters had arrived.' He looked across the room. 'You were with her, Laura.'

Without looking up his sister said, 'What's that?'

'You saw Deirdre off on the day she met her end.'

'I don't think so.'

'I'm sorry, my dear. As the inspector says, this might be important. You did see her off. I remember it clearly. I was embarrassed. Your voices were raised. You must remember.'

'I don't.'

'I saw you from the window,' Jameson persisted. 'You followed her to the car. She jumped in and drove off fast.'

'If you say so, William.'

Cook picked up Jameson's words. 'So she drove off fast?'

'Yes.'

'Didn't take her time. Settle into her seat. Fasten her seat belt. Look around?'

'Nothing like that. The door slammed and she was away.'

'And so,' Cook went on, the measured tread of his voice like a policeman on a slow beat, 'it is conceivable that she wouldn't have known whether someone was hiding in the back of the car.'

Jameson frowned. 'Conceivable, yes, but unlikely.'

'Why unlikely? It's a large car. Plenty of room in the back.'

Jameson said nothing.

'According to the gentleman she met at the Cock Inn,' Cook continued, 'she hurried from the car when she arrived. She was already very late for their date. It seems quite plausible that she could have travelled there with a passenger, unknown to her, hiding in the back. The same passenger could have climbed into the front and followed her with her gentleman friend. He could have parked near the wood, intercepted her when she ran from the gentleman's car, killed her and driven back. But, instead of leaving the car at the Cock Inn, as he should have done, to cover his tracks, he drove it to Ipswich. Perhaps time was short for him. He may have needed to get back to wherever he'd come from as soon as possible in case his absence was noticed. Or perhaps he simply didn't think about leaving the car at the place where he had taken it over.'

Jameson considered the hypothesis. 'As you say, it's speculation.'

'Still in the field of speculation,' Cook went on, 'and bearing in mind that there were no unaccountable fingerprints in the car, I have to say that a great number of the prints were of your gardener, Daryll Lee.'

Jameson recovered some of his spirit. 'Not surprising, is it? Daryll sometimes drove the car and he cleans both cars.'

'Not in the least surprising. Did you know, sir, that your employee has a criminal record?'

The clicking needles were suddenly silent.

Jameson shifted in his seat. 'I knew. Of course I knew. He was quite open about it. But I believe in helping people, as does my sister. We both believe in helping the disadvantaged. Lame dogs over stiles.' His voice became firm. 'Of course I knew he had a record. But employment opportunities are difficult in this area and he needed all the help he could get.'

'Did you know the record was of violence? Grievous bodily harm? Attempted rape?'

'I knew. But all human beings are redeemable.'

'I mention it,' said Cook, 'because we were aware from the start that your gardener, Mr Lee, could be a suspect. We interviewed him, as you must know, but although he has Thursdays as his days off, and can come and go as he wishes, he had an alibi. Two friends, gypsies, swear he spent the afternoon drinking with them. I have always been sceptical of this alibi but I couldn't shake it. However, the situation has changed.'

'Are you saying . . .' Jameson left the sentence unfinished.

'I'm not saying anything more than I have said. But I have another question. Has your man, Lee, got a sweet tooth?'

Jameson blinked. 'Sweet tooth?'

'Sweet tooth. Does he like confections?'

'Now that you mention it, yes.'

'Have you ever seen him eating a Mars bar? You know what Mars bars are?'

'Certainly I do. And yes, he does have a particular weakness for them. That's right, isn't it, Laura?'

Laura Jameson stood up. 'I have work to do,' she said in a strained voice. 'Excuse me.' She dropped the knitting on her chair.

Cook also stood up. 'Just a moment, madam. Before you go, what part did you play in all this?'

'I don't know what you mean.'

Cook barred her way. 'I think you do.'

'William, tell these men to go.'

Jameson now stood up. Only Detective Sergeant Pinkney was seated and, as if feeling it improper to remain on a chair while others were standing, he too stood.

'You are upsetting my sister,' said Jameson.

190

'I'm sorry, sir, but a lot of people have been distressed by this case. Can you tell me where Mr Lee is at this moment?'

'He's where he should be. In the garden somewhere.'

'And is he, Miss Jameson?' Cook asked quietly. 'Or is he upstairs?'

To the surprise of Detective Sergeant Pinkney she covered her face with her hands and began crying with a keening wail.

'I don't like Cook,' said Rodney, 'but he's not a bad detective.'

They were in the sitting room of their home in north London. Max, his leg scarred and stiff, was asleep by Stella's feet. In the background music was playing on the radio. They were waiting for the newscast to find out whether the jury had yet reached a verdict in a trial which had become sensational reader-fodder for the tabloids. Daryll Lee had been accused of the murder of the attractive and wayward Deirdre Jameson but in defence had claimed that the death was accidental. He had only been trying to frighten Deirdre and was doing so at the request of William Jameson's sister who wanted Deirdre out of the house.

Under pressure from prosecuting counsel he admitted he had made advances to Deirdre and been rebuffed. There was a stir of excitement in the public gallery when he went on to say, 'But Mr Jameson's sister put me up to it. She said unless I did as I was told she'd tell her brother about some stuff of his she'd seen me nick. It didn't stop there. I had to satisfy her . . .' At this point the judge had interrupted and instructed the jury to ignore this hearsay.

As the trial progressed a picture emerged of a jealous woman who regarded Deirdre as her rival and wanted to get rid of her and used a not very bright gardener to achieve her ends.

191

The music on the radio faded. A time signal. The news-reader's voice. Three items of international interest and then the item Rodney and Stella had been waiting for. 'A short while ago we learned that the jury has found Daryll Lee guilty of murder of . . .'

'Thank God that's over,' said Rodney.

'. . . the trial judge has deferred sentence until tomorrow.'

'Or almost over,' he added.

'In a way,' said Stella, 'although he was guilty, no doubt of that, the sister shares the guilt and she got off scot-free.'

'If what he said was true. He could have been lying to save his skin. To get a lesser sentence. If there'd been anything provable she'd have been charged as an accessory.'

'At least Dad didn't get dragged in.'

He switched off the radio.

'But things will never be the same again,' she went on. 'It's not just the cottage. Okay, we'll sell it. But something else has been lost.' After a pause she said, 'I think what's been lost is something to do with peace of mind.'